20

WHE
WE W
FAM

WHEN WE WUZ FAMOUS

GREG TAKOUDES

Christy Ottaviano Books
Henry Holt and Company   New York

Henry Holt and Company, LLC
Publishers since 1866
175 Fifth Avenue
New York, New York 10010
macteenbooks.com

Library of Congress Cataloging-in-Publication Data
Takoudes, Greg.
When we wuz famous / Greg Takoudes. — 1st ed.
p.   cm.
Summary: Novel adaptation of the author's feature film, "Up with me."
ISBN 978-0-8050-9452-7 (hardcover)
 I. Up with me (Motion picture).   II. Title.
PZ7.T141375Whe 2013
[Fic]—dc23

                                    2012027733

First Edition—2013 / Designed by Ashley Halsey
Printed in the United States of America

10 9 8 7 6 5 4 3 2 1

For Emily,
who deserves this and more, and more, and more

WHEN
WE WUZ
FAMOUS

PART ONE

SPANISH HARLEM

1

Are you ready to hear it?

Let's begin by saying what this story is *not*. For starters, it's not crap. That's not to say this story is necessarily any good—it's just not packed with lies. It's not about a bunch of perfect-looking teenagers who dance around in designer outfits, stage pillow fights, and deliver the perfect, rip-roaring comeback to every insult. Nope. This is a story about real kids. Actual kids. Kids you like, kids you love, kids you hate—the types of kids you know.

Now, *technically*, you would have to call this a love story, as much as it might make your skin crawl. But it's not the kind of love story *you're* thinking of. No one buys chocolate valentines for anyone in this story. So if you're looking for that heartwarming (and stomach-curdling) scene where the varsity boy surprises his blond girlfriend with a bouquet of flowers and balloons on her birthday after she'd positively *feared* that he'd forgotten, then it's time to put this book down and start reading another one.

That scene is not in this book.

In fact, this is the kind of story where the boy actually does forget it's his girl's birthday, because he's an idiot, and she really needs to dump his ass, and all her friends tell her so. But she won't. Because she's being an idiot too. Because that's what happens in real life. The subtitle of this book should be *The Stupid Stuff That People Do, and Why They Keep Doing It.*

Another thing: Don't expect the characters you're about to meet to do things like *learn important lessons in life.* This isn't some CW television show where the characters get to *learn about themselves* just in the nick of time before the show has to cut to a commercial that's selling you fabric softener.

No, this book is about real love. And the thing about real love is that it hurts. You don't get real love without going through real problems first. Infatuation ain't love. Great sex ain't love. Flowers on your birthday ain't love. Those things are nice, but they aren't true love. The thing about true love is that you have to get through a lot of junk—lies, pain, dishonesty—and then you have to somehow survive it all before you can get to the good part: the love that lasts.

So are you ready to hear it?

Oh, and one more thing. This book is a bit strange, too, because for a love story, it starts in the least romantic place in the world: a police station. And for a love story, it starts with the least romantic topic of conversation you can imagine: murder.

June 28

Whether you want to admit it or not, it's a well-known fact that girls are smarter than boys. Girls are probably more interesting, too. So if this is gonna be a halfway good story, then it has to start with a girl. If we started with a boy, then nothing would happen. The book would begin and end with some kid sitting on his couch playing Xbox. Sometimes boys need a kick in the butt to get off the couch and get anything done. Boys need girls like the space shuttle needs a booster engine, and for a story that's this crazy, we need an engine as fast and cool as a girl named Reignbow Rivera.

Now, Reignbow runs with a crew called the Kaos Krew. The Krew's made up of six friends, three boys and three girls. We'll get a chance to meet all of them and hear everything that happened in one roller-coaster year of their lives. It was a year that changed all of them. Some for the better, some for the worse. And some for the *much* worse. We'll sort it all out in the end.

Anyway, let's begin with what we have so far: Reignbow, a police station, and a murder. It's June. Reignbow sits in a gray concrete interrogation room in the Ninety-second Police Precinct of Spanish Harlem. Take a close look at her face while she listens to some female cop droning on. Reign's tired eyes fight to stay awake, her locked jaw bites her tongue to keep from lashing out, and her pinched eyebrows resent having to be here. But unlike most girls who have to dredge themselves in makeup like chickens through batter in order to get a second look, Reignbow's natural beauty never leaves her. She is voluptuous at her hips and chest, with big brown eyes and a knowing smile. The longer you look at her, the prettier she gets. She's the kind of girl whose beauty sneaks up on you, a girl who gets noticed eventually . . . who gets asked out by the right guy, eventually . . . because she knows, eventually, that good things come to those who wait.

And so she waits.

In a gray concrete interrogation room.

How does a girl like this wind up in a police station? Even Reignbow isn't sure. She doesn't know how long the police will keep her here or how much trouble she's actually in or, really, *anything* about what happened in the park tonight—that dark, forested park where only drug dealers and prostitutes ever go at night—that led to the killing of a boy she's known her whole life, and led to her sitting in this room.

Sitting across the table from Reignbow is the cop. A tough, female NYPD cop, Caucasian, freckled complexion, and strawberry hair pulled back into a tight bun. The cop's expression is icy; her demeanor is severe. This cop clearly doesn't want people to see that she's mildly pretty. All she wants people to see is her badge. Number 3286. Keating, Molly. Detective rank.

3

Detective Keating pours a cup of water and slides it across the aluminum table. Reignbow doesn't move.

"Not thirsty?"

Reignbow eyes the water suspiciously. "No."

"You can go look at the vending machine if you're hungry—"

"I can get my own food at home, thank you very much. I don't want your cop water. Probably poisoned."

Detective Keating tilts her head. "Why in the world would we poison your water?"

"I don't know. I don't even know why you dragged me in here."

"It's because we want some answers."

"So I'm in trouble?"

"Not exactly."

"Then I can leave?"

"You're free to go whenever you want. Go home and eat your own unpoisoned food from your own kitchen."

"For real?"

"For real. But I recommend that you don't leave, Ms. Rivera. I think you should stay."

"Why?"

"Because a friend of yours was killed tonight, and now you have two choices. You can stay and help us find the killers, or you can leave and help the killers get away. Do you see what I mean?"

"I guess . . ." Her words trail off into the air. She rubs her eyes. "What time is it?"

"Two or two thirty in the morning."

"This is crazy."

"I know. But you have to understand," says the detective, "we can't just run out and catch the bad guys. We're going to need help. Your help. It's the right thing to do."

It may be the right thing, and even *the good thing*, but there's one thing that a smart girl like Reignbow knows, and it's that old saying about how no good deed goes unpunished.

"Listen, I don't really know anything," says Reignbow. "I only heard about the shooting from what everyone else was saying. It's not like I was even there."

"I understand that. But you did know the principals involved, correct?"

"Principals?"

"The victims. And the assailants. Am I correct that you knew the people on both sides?"

"What? No. Why would I know the killers?"

Detective Keating opens a file and looks through some notes. "It's here in your file——"

"It's in the file or it's in your head?"

"Excuse me?"

"I know how you cops think. You look at someone like me and you assume: Young plus Hispanic equals troublemakers, right?"

"Did I say any of that?" says Detective Keating, looking offended.

"You might as well have. What do you think, I hang out with criminals? I don't know any criminals!"

"Ms. Rivera."

"What?" Reignbow barks.

"I think we're getting off on the wrong foot. I know you're upset—"

"You don't know shit."

Silence engulfs the room. For the first time, Reignbow hears voices from the next room. The voices are faint, but she can hear a man yelling and a woman crying. The woman sounds like she's pleading. Reignbow gets a shiver down her spine.

The detective clears her throat. "Let's begin this way: Tell me about your relationship with Vincent."

Reignbow shrugs. "Vincent? Me and him never got along. What do you want to know?"

"Well, *why* didn't you get along?"

" 'Cause he's the craziest boy you ever met. Anyone would say that."

"So you didn't like him because he was crazy?"

"Of course not. *All* my friends are crazy. But with Vincent, it's different. There's crazy fun, and then there's crazy crazy. You know what I mean?"

"I do."

"Vincent and I fought like dogs, and usually the fights were about Francisco. Vincent is Francisco's oldest friend, but I'm Francisco's girlfriend. So, you know, it was like a stupid jealousy thing. F acted bad whenever he was around Vincent. You ever see those pictures of a guy with a devil on one shoulder and an angel on the other?"

"Sure."

"Well, Vincent was the devil. And I was the angel. Or I tried to be."

Detective Keating opens another file. "Vincent's got quite a lengthy record. Nothing big, but it's consistent." She picks out the top page. "Last time we saw him was seven months ago, for breaking into a car." She puts the page down. "Francisco's record is clean. Why would he be best friends with such a bad egg?"

" 'Cause it's more complicated than you think. Vincent's and Francisco's moms are second cousins, or some kinda relation. Vincent's mom was seriously messed up." Reignbow touches her head. "Mental." Then she touches the inside of her elbow, along the veins. "Too much of this, you know what I mean? One second, she'd be like this perfect loving mom to Vincent, and the next second, she's high and kicking him outta the house. Her mind was all warped and stupid from those drugs. Vincent was just a little kid, but his mom didn't care; she used to boot his ass out to the streets. He was maybe seven, or six. Or even younger. Folks in the neighborhood used to spot Vincent walkin' around at all hours and call Francisco's mom, and she would come pick him up. She'd bring that little boy back to her apartment and give him a meal, a bath. You can't help but feel sorry for Vincent just thinkin' about it." Reignbow pauses. "I mean, no one's got the right to treat other people like shit, but if anyone's got half an excuse for doing it, it's Vincent."

Detective Keating makes a quick note in the file. "Okay, so Vincent, troubled childhood. Got it."

Reignbow looks up, surprised. "What?"

"Let's move on."

"Did you say you *got* it?"

"Yes."

"I don't think you do. I'm telling you about a little kid who's homeless in the streets, and all you can say is, I got it?"

"What do you want me to say?"

"What's it say on your copmobiles parked outside? *C-P-R.* Courtesy. Professionalism. Respect. Right? You ever read that? Where's the respect?"

"Ms. Rivera, this isn't exactly the first time I've heard a story like this. What should I do, break down and cry over your friend? I couldn't be a detective if I did."

"The fact is, you just don't care at all," Reignbow nearly yells. "That's the whole problem with you cops. You open up shop in *our* neighborhood and walk around like *you* own it. Meanwhile the whole neighborhood's falling apart, but you cops do nothing to stop it!"

"Ms. Rivera—"

"Did you know there's a stoplight on my block that's been broke for a year now? There's no red light, no green light. Cars just go through the intersection whenever they want, and a few months ago, a girl who lives in my building got hit. But where were you cops then? Where was your help when that little girl was hit?"

Detective Keating doesn't answer; she doesn't even blink. She stares at Reignbow with a cold, long stare that eventually pushes Reignbow back into her seat. Shame fills Reign's cheeks until she's full-on blushing. She's not much of a yeller, and her mom would kill her for yelling at a cop. It just isn't her.

"Are you finished?" says the detective.

Reignbow nods and looks at her hands. She folds them into her pockets and wishes the rest of her could disappear, too.

"Good," says the detective. "Because my time is very limited. So we're going to switch topics . . . *without* you yelling. All right?"

Reignbow nods again.

"Now, tell me about Francisco."

Reignbow's voice is nearly a whisper. "What do you want to know?"

"When's the last time you saw him?"

Reignbow shrugs. "Seven months ago?"

"That's a long time to go without seeing your boyfriend."

"So?"

"Did you have a fight? Does it have anything to do with the shooting tonight?"

"A fight? You could say that." Reignbow tries to remember, but it hurts too much. It hurts because she's spent the last six months trying to forget it all.

"I dunno. Hard to say exactly. It's complicated. . . ."

"I'm sure it is. But it sounds like it's related."

"Maybe."

"So tell me."

Reignbow swallows hard, like swallowing a jawbreaker. "The thing about Francisco . . . and the murder tonight. See, it might all be my fault."

"*Your* fault?"

"It's a long story."

Detective Keating gives Reignbow a level gaze. "Ms. Rivera, it's very important that you tell me everything. It's crucial to the case. And it's crucial to catching the killers."

"Okay, I'll tell you. But what happens if you determine that it really *was* all my fault?"

"I can't say right now. I don't know the answer until you tell me. I'm going to have to hear all of it to understand—everything, from the beginning."

Nine months earlier: September 3

Francisco pressed his face against the window of his bedroom, peering eighteen stories down to a trash-strewn alleyway with overflowing Dumpsters. Past the edge of his building, he could see the Harlem River, and beyond it, the parks on Randall's Island. When you grow up in the inner city there aren't many scenic views, but Francisco had one. Or at least a sliver of a view, down to that river and those parks. The water sparkled brilliantly in the setting sun.

He imagined a real estate brochure advertising his family's apartment: *Only blocks away from dealers peddling your drug of choice! Enjoy the views of the river without being close enough to smell the garbage floating on it!*

Francisco turned away from the window, a smile on his lips. Part of him was *very* happy to be leaving New York.

He picked up a basketball trophy. It was one of those hulking, impressive ones that you can hold above your head and pump up and down to cheering crowds. Francisco won the trophy just a few months ago, when he led his basketball squad to the regional championships. Francisco was named the MVP of the season. It was the first time in eight years that a junior had won MVP. He could still hear the cheering in his ears, standing there alone in his room. He put down the trophy and picked up a framed certificate from the wall. *Francisco Ortiz—High Honor Roll—Luis W. Alvarez High School.* He won that last year, too.

It was the best year of his life.

His successes earned him the attention of the school principal, Dr. Tyson, who called Francisco into his office one day and asked him if he'd ever thought about his future. A future beyond the streets of Spanish Harlem.

"Have you ever imagined yourself," said Dr. Tyson, an educated black man with a deep voice and huge hands that seemed to be grasping at wondrous ideas floating through the air, "finishing your high school career at one of the best schools in the country?"

Dr. Tyson paused dramatically.

"You mean Urban Academy in Washington Heights?"

"No, no, no," said Dr. Tyson. He pushed a glossy brochure in front of Francisco, and opened each fold like it was the Ark of the Covenant. Francisco looked at the pictures of long grassy lawns, ivy-covered buildings, and students dressed in coats and ties. Across the top of the brochure was written "Seton Grove Academy—*ad astra per aspera.*"

"Is that French?" asked Francisco, thinking French was always used for fancy stuff and this school looked pretty fancy.

"Latin. It means 'to the stars through difficulty.' And I think, Francisco, that you're on your way up."

That meeting didn't seem so long ago. And now Francisco was pulling his one nice blazer and tie out of the closet, rolling them up, and slipping them into his oversized duffel bag. He was ready to join those kids from the brochure. To walk those lawns. To live in those ivy-covered dormitories.

He zipped the duffel closed and looked around his room one last time. It looked pretty well cleared out, but he was surprised how little stuff he'd packed. There was just one oversized sagging duffel bag and a backpack at his feet, like a comedy duo: the fat guy and the tiny guy. Surely he must own more stuff than this? He went back into his drawers and dug around, pulling out his two favorite hoodies. One said NEW YORK ORIGINAL in graffiti letters; another had a stencil of Scarface holding a machine gun. SAY 'ELLO TO MY LEETLE FRIEND.

These clothes used to be his uniform. He thought about the pictures from Dr. Tyson's slickly colored pamphlet. There were white kids sitting in classrooms. White kids playing tennis. Black and Latino kids were occasionally featured here or there, but they dressed just like the white kids.

He took another look at Scarface and scowled. There wasn't a single hoodie in all those pictures. He could barely find anyone wearing jeans. The kids looked like models for Lacoste ads.

Francisco stuffed Scarface back into the drawer and closed it. One duffel and one backpack it would have to be, then. He stared at the two pathetic bags, the silent comedy duo, waiting for them to tell him a joke. Francisco kicked the duffel, knocking a large frown in its side. He'd never been so nervous in his life.

The ceramic positively glowed. Viviana scrubbed with such fervor that a pair of yellow stains, which had been living unwanted in the kitchen sink of this modest two-bedroom apartment for thirty years, finally vanished into her scrub brush.

Francisco watched his mother from the hallway, biting his lip. Cleaning meant she was anxious. Scrubbing the toilet meant she was nervous about money. Scrubbing the floors meant she was nervous about her health. And scrubbing the kitchen sink meant she was nervous about Francisco.

Needless to say, the apartment was always immaculate.

"Hey, Ma, you doing okay?"

"Oh, Francisco!" she said, flashing a surprised smile. "I didn't see you there." She brushed her hair to the side with the back of her yellow plastic glove. Francisco could see that she'd been crying. "Yes, I'm fine."

"All right. Well, I gotta go now. I'll be back later."

"Where you going?"

"I got to see Reign and stuff. Got to say my good-byes."

"Oh, my baby." She reached up and grabbed her son, sniffling into his chest. She could barely reach her arms around his enormous shoulders. He'd only turned twelve when he sprouted above her head. At fifteen, he had passed his dad. He'd still been growing this past year. It didn't take much imagination to look at his LeBron-like frame and think he might have talent on the basketball court.

"Do you have everything you need? Are you packed?"

"Yes."

"Do you have enough warm clothes?"

"Uh-huh."

"Do you have your train ticket?"

"Yes, Ma."

"Okay, good." She tapped her gloved finger to her forehead like she'd forgotten something to ask him, depositing a soap bubble on her eyebrow. An empty thought bubble. Francisco wiped it away for her. Then she remembered. "I was meaning to ask you about food. Should I pack you food? What will you eat up there?"

"They serve food up there. At the school. We've been over this." Her concern for him was sweet, but a little exasperating.

"Are you sure? Did you ask them about it?"

"No . . . but of course they're going to have food. I mean, what do any of the kids eat? Everyone lives in the dorms. They have to eat somewhere."

"Ah, yes, but what kind of food? Will they serve *arroz con pollo*? That's your favorite."

"No, Ma. They don't serve Puerto Rican food. They serve, I don't know . . . white kids' food."

His mother screwed up her face and looked sick. "What is that? French fries?"

"Ma, I'll be fine. Okay? Don't worry so much about me. I'm more worried about you and Pop."

She shook her head and took off her gloves. "Oh, we'll be fine. Don't make me worry about you worrying about me. It'll just give me something else to worry about! Now go, go."

"Okay." Francisco paused. "Is Pop around? My train is so early, I don't know if I'll see him in the morning."

"He's in the bedroom. You can go in if you want."

Francisco peered down the hall. The bedroom door was closed. Francisco could hear the fast notes of Telemundo news coming through the walls.

"Go ahead," she said.

"No, I don't want to disturb him. . . ."

Viviana saw the disappointment on Francisco's face. "Francisco."

"Look, I'm already gonna be late for Reign."

"Your father's going to miss you, you know."

"I know."

"Just as much as I will."

"Really?"

"Yes. You know your father. He feels it." She pointed to her heart. "He just doesn't want to say it."

"But it's like he doesn't say anything to me. All summer. Ever since I got accepted. Is he mad I'm leaving?"

"Of course not! He loves you, Francisco. He's so proud of you. You just have to believe it, even if you can't see it."

Francisco shrugged. His phone vibrated, and he checked the message.

"It's Reign. She's already there. I should go."

Viviana hugged Francisco one more time. He saw in her face that she was trying to be brave. "Ma . . ."

"Go ahead," she said. "We'll be okay."

He went out the door. The elevator was all the way at the other end of the hall. He ran past fifty apartments before he got to the elevator. Passing each door, he heard couples screaming and fighting, TVs blaring, some couple having sex, and hip-hop thumping. But no matter how far he got, no matter how fast he ran, and no matter how loud the rest of the noise was, Francisco could still hear his mother's quiet sobbing.

Francisco checked his watch while he ran through the streets, dodging cars and people. It was a compulsion he'd picked up a couple months ago, ever since the madness of going off to boarding school started. Checking his watch every hour. And sometimes every minute.

The last few months had been a house of mirrors of endless tasks to complete, with every direction he turned revealing a new set of deadlines and obligations. The Seton Grove application itself was a bear to finish on time—writing the essays, gathering his transcript and his teachers' recommendations, all the while keeping up with basketball and his own schoolwork. Once he got accepted, his schedule only got worse. He had financial aid forms to fill out and then it seemed like there were a million people he had to tell about getting into boarding school: relatives, friends, neighbors. He had packing to do, clothes to buy, books to find online and order. It was almost too much to stay on top of, and so he found himself waking up in the middle of the night in a panic, sitting up in bed, checking his watch.

Still, he was late for everything. He was even late for Reignbow. Sprinting down Lexington Avenue, past 105th Street, he took a left turn through a hidden gate that few people who'd lived in Spanish Harlem all their lives even knew existed.

On the other side of the gate, he found himself in another world. He ran across a gravel pathway, through flowers and bushes. His footsteps landed near tiny stone cherubs that were poking out of the bushes. He leapt over a babbling brook and spotted Reignbow standing in the middle of a wooden footbridge. She was looking down into the brook, lost in her thoughts. The stream wasn't real—the water came from a buried hose—but nevertheless, the sounds of the city seemed to fade away inside this place, a nearly magical oasis in the center of the inner city. Nestled in between the back lots and alleys of dirty old apartment buildings soaring above it, Hope Park was Francisco and Reignbow's favorite spot. It was the place they came when they first started dating, almost a year ago. It was the place where they had shared their first kiss.

Francisco ran up the bridge, and Reignbow smiled.

"I was wondering if you was ever going to get here," she said. He pulled her into a hug, and Reignbow leaned into his chest. He held her tightly, keeping her warm from the evening's cooling breeze. They stayed quiet like that, hugging for a while.

"What's wrong, chatterbox?" he finally asked, pulling away. Her face was serene. "You're quiet as a mouse."

"I don't know. . . ." She tried to smile for him, but it looked more like a frown. "Can I ask you something, F?"

"Of course."

"What's going to happen to us after you leave?"

"Nothing's going to happen. Everything's going to stay the same."

"You ain't gonna break up with me?"

"What? No way."

"You promise?"

"Of course," said Francisco. "I promise . . . I promise."

Whenever he talked, he talked close, and he talked certain. His confidence calmed her. She felt his warm breath slip down her shirt like a hand. She'd never liked someone this much. She'd never loved anyone so much. To have those feelings wrapped into one guy left her awake at nights, heart racing, eyes wet, thinking about him.

He promised again—even quieter. *"Nothing will happen."*

Behind them there was a mural. There were murals all over Spanish Harlem, but most were shrines to rappers or memorials to dead teenagers. The mural in this park was of a pastoral world far beyond the city's limits, of great flowing rivers and mountains and endless farms—places Reignbow imagined she'd never get to see, so she was happy to have them here.

"The thing is, Francisco, you're moving upstate, and you know, when you're far away, anything can happen."

"Anything like what?"

"Like, you could meet a skinny, blond, rich white girl and . . . you know . . . do that thing."

"Do *what* thing?"

Reignbow leveled her eyes at him. "What thing d'you think I'm talking about?"

"I don't know. There's a lot of things."

She laughed.

"I'm not going to do any*thing* with any*one*, Reignbow."

"Good. And you're going to always text me, right?"

"Of course."

"You're going to always call?"

"Sure."

"You're not gonna come back to visit like a white boy, are you? With suspenders and glasses, and walking all doofy with your . . . English proper, are you?"

"Look at me," Francisco said. She did, but slowly. Shyly. "Is there any way that an inner-city kid could come back with suspenders?" he said.

"Anything's possible—"

"And glasses—"

"*Anything* is possible. That's what I'm talking about!"

"Yeah, but not in this 'hood."

She laughed. "True. I mean, you would get jumped."

He laughed, too. But the realization kept hitting him: Tomorrow morning, he was going to leave her. Leave everything. Family, friends, and every last person he'd ever met in his life.

"Francisco, let's get out of here. Come over to my place, you know?" She tugged at his shirt playfully.

"Now?"

"Yeah."

"Yo, I'd love to. But I can't tonight."

"Why not?" Her face fell.

"I gotta . . ." He checked his watch. That compulsive thing. " 'Cause I gotta see Vincent. I didn't have a chance to say good-bye to him before."

Reignbow bristled. Vincent: the third member of the Krew. He was the clown, the playboy, and he was pure trouble. Reignbow looked off into the distance and pushed back the urge to feel jealous.

"Believe me, I wish I had the whole night for you," he said. "Next time, all right?"

"All right."

"I love you, you know that?"

"I do."

She closed her eyes and kissed him, and when she opened them, darkness had come. The towers' lights turned on, and the hundreds of apartments above them filled with noises and the smell of dinners cooking. A parks employee came into the park with keys and shooed them out. The park was closing for the night. The worker turned off the hose that fed water into the little stream. Francisco and Reignbow walked out together and emerged into the noisy streets of Spanish Harlem, where taxis honked and homeless people screamed at no one, and the peacefulness of the park faded far, far behind them.

After dropping off Reignbow at her apartment, Francisco sprinted through the city streets. All kinds of people were out. Families on an evening stroll, mobs of kids laughing and shouting. The streets were, as always, alive with love and fury and adventure. Francisco didn't know much about the boarding school he'd be attending, but he knew it wouldn't be like Spanish Harlem. It was going to be quiet up there. The kind of place that had more trees than people.

Vincent was already waiting for Francisco at the Harlem River pier, leaning against an iron fence and looking out at the gigantic, twinkling river. Vincent looked sad as hell.

"Hey. Sorry I'm late," said Francisco, rushing up.

"I've been here since eight. Where was you?"

"With Reignbow. I lost track of time." He wiped the sweat off his forehead. "This is really hard on her."

Vincent shrugged. "So what? She's the only one this is hard for?"

Vincent had movie star good looks. He had angry, sensitive eyes that would have given him credible movie roles as a thug or an altar boy. Francisco leaned up next to him and they were silent for a while as he went into his thoughts about all the things he'd miss from here.

"So this is it, huh?" said Vincent. "Good-bye."

"Yeah. But only for a little bit."

"You really gonna do this, Fran? You gonna bounce on us?"

"It isn't like that—"

"Yeah, it is! You're bouncing on your boys and your whole neighborhood. I mean, Spanish Harlem where you from. Not upstate. Only white motherfuckers upstate."

Vincent spat into the river and watched the mighty loogie soar. They stood at a pier on 112th Street on the east side of Manhattan. This was *their* pier, just like Francisco and Reignbow had their own park. The pier was halfway between their respective Harlems—black and Spanish. The lights of Long Island City shimmered like confetti in the Harlem River.

"You gonna play basketball up there?"

"I told them I would."

"Then your squad probably hate you, too."

"Why d'you say that?"

"You carried them to regionals last year. They don't have a prayer of doing it again. You just gonna go win for some other team now."

"C'mon. What am I supposed to do? Stay in the 'hood just so we can get another championship? I want more than that."

"Yeah? Like what? To be some kind of inner-city inspiration? Become 'the kid who escaped the 'hood'? You want to wind up on *Oprah* or some shit? If you leave where you're from, then all you're doing is messing things up."

Nearby, some old men were fishing for bass. It was a tradition around here. Fishermen hauled the fish out of the river and threw them into *I Heart NY* plastic bags filled with ice. The fish slapped around inside the bags, choking to death on air. City officials put up signs along the pier warning people not to eat the fish because of the pollution in the river, but folks cooked them up and ate them anyway.

"What are you gonna do long term, Fran? Stay upstate? Go to college up there? Where that gonna leave Reignbow?"

"What do you care about Reignbow?"

"I don't. But you do. You know what this is gonna do to her?"

Francisco nodded. He knew. He just didn't want to think about it.

"You gotta remember the good times, Fran. How we chill, man; be you, me, the Krew chillin' around the neighborhood. We all over Spanish Harlem. Yo, our Krew's world famous in this 'hood. You feel me?"

"I feel you. I do—"

"Yo, I don't wanna *miss* those days."

"Yeah, but then what are you saying? That you're always going to stay in the 'hood?"

Vincent clapped his hands. "Hell, yeah! I'm the same old Vincent, ruling the same old 'hood—I ain't never gonna change!"

He jumped up onto the top of the iron fence, balancing himself precariously, and called out to the streets, "Harlem is *me*, man! This place is mine!" His voice lost itself in the busy streets. He cupped his hands around his mouth and yelled, "See me on the block, yo!"

"Get your ass off there before you fall in the river, fool." Francisco grabbed Vincent's arms and pulled him back down to the street. "Chill the hell out."

Vincent leaned against the fence again and shook his head sorrowfully. "Shit, Fran, everything's gonna get all fucked up now. We all just gonna split up 'cause of you. Where's the Krew gonna be at?"

"The Krew will still be together, man. I'll be back on school breaks. You'll see me when I'm around."

"See you around, huh? That ain't what I'm talkin' about. I'm talking about how everything's changing. The whole world is. I hate it."

"Believe me, I'll be thinking about Harlem all the time. That's all I'll be thinking about is y'all."

Vincent turned his head and fumed. "It better be." The river below the pier ran on and on. Vincent wondered how something so big as this river could run so silently. He wondered if the water would ever run out. "You my brother, Fran. I just got to tell you that before you go and disappear on me, ai'ight?"

"Ai'ight. I'm gonna miss you, Vin. I'm gonna miss all of this."

Francisco could see across the river, all the way to Long Island City in Queens. He could see the Navy Yard in Brooklyn and the high-wire tram crossing the black sky toward Roosevelt Island. Down along Manhattan, he saw the United Nations building, flat like a remote control. It was a beautiful, busy night. A typical city night. It was Francisco's last night in Spanish Harlem.

Some folks called Vincent CIA, because you never could quite figure him out. The boy was loaded with secrets, and nothing he did made much sense. Even Francisco couldn't figure him out. It was only fitting that when Francisco first met him, he actually thought Vincent was a ghost. They'd been friends for months before Francisco realized Vincent wasn't just a figment of his imagination, an imaginary best friend.

The whole thing started when Francisco was a little kid, plagued by nightmares. He used to wake up in the middle of the night with terrible visions of army tanks rolling over him, volcanoes exploding and burning him, his parents abandoning him in the street and never coming back. He just could not switch off his mind.

But when he turned five, the violent images in Francisco's head seemed to disappear, and he started having one dream: of a boy, not much older than himself, asleep on his floor. Next to tanks and volcanoes, the presence of this softly snoring little ghost was almost calming, and eventually Francisco would turn over and go back to sleep. By the next morning, under the glare of the new day's sun, the boy was always gone.

The dream seemed to return every few nights, until one night when curiosity got the better of Francisco. Was it possible that this was really the *same* dream? Was it even a dream at all?

As a test, while he was having the dream, Francisco pinched himself on the arm. But he didn't wake up. Or rather, he must have already been awake. So he got out of bed and tiptoed across the room, wondering if maybe he'd somehow fallen into *this* boy's dream. Quietly pulling down the boy's sleeping bag until the fleshy part of his arm was exposed, Francisco gave the kid a hard, nasty pinch.

The boy jumped up. "What are you doing?"

"What are *you* doing?" yelled Francisco, stumbling back to his bed.

"You woke me up!"

"I'm sorry, but what are you doing in here?"

"Sleeping, fool."

"Are you a ghost?"

The little boy shivered and pulled the sleeping bag up again. "I sometimes feel like I am."

"Where're you from?"

The boy pointed out the window. "Up a ways. Uptown."

Francisco pointed straight up. "You mean like, *up* up? You're an angel?"

"Huh?" The boy looked off into the darkness of the room. The strangeness of the conversation made him woozy, and he lay back down. "Yo, I'm going back to sleep now."

Francisco watched as the boy started snoring a few seconds later.

The next morning at breakfast with his parents, Francisco slurped his bowl of Cheerios and thought about the boy. He wondered if he was indeed an angel—perhaps Francisco's guardian angel, protecting him from his nightmares. And that's when Viviana announced that someone would be coming to live with them. She explained about a distant cousin of hers who was always in trouble from drinking and drugging. This cousin lived in Central Harlem, which was also called Black Harlem, up on 135th Street, thirty blocks north of Spanish Harlem. The drugging habit was so bad that this cousin couldn't even raise her own child, so Viviana had persuaded her to go into rehab and get clean, and while she was going to be away, they'd look after her son. The boy's name was Vincent.

Francisco swallowed a big spoonful of cereal. "Is he bringing toys?"

Viviana smiled. "I don't know. But I want you to share yours with him. Be nice to him."

Francisco nodded and went back to his cereal.

An hour later, there was a knock. Viviana opened the door to her rail-thin cousin. The woman was hunched and had drooping red eyes and missing teeth. Next to her was—of all people—the imaginary boy from Francisco's room. Francisco stared at him as his mother and the strung-out lady talked. When the lady left, Viviana grabbed the boy's hand to bring him inside, and when her hand didn't go right through the boy's hand, that's when Francisco knew he was made of flesh and blood.

Along with being real, the boy was painfully shy. Viviana told Francisco, "Go get Vincent those toys, would you?"

But Francisco just stared at him and couldn't move. "*He* can find 'em," he whispered.

Viviana ushered Vincent toward Francisco's bedroom, and the boy disappeared inside.

"You recognize him, huh?" said Viviana.

"Yeah."

"I tried to be as quiet as possible whenever I brought him in. I'd get calls in the middle of the night. Vincent would be out in the streets somewhere, his mom gone off. She always came back early the next morning to pick him up, though. Apologizing like crazy. Saying it would never happen again. Of course, it always did."

Viviana knelt down and hugged Francisco. "We got to take care of Vincent now. He's our responsibility till his mom comes back. Okay?"

"Okay."

"Now, go play with him. Make sure he's not lonely. As hard as this is on us, it's much harder for him."

Francisco went into his room, where Vincent was already on the floor next to an open bin of Legos. He was building a tower. Francisco found a Star Wars fighter pod and circled the tower a few times, then flew in and crashed it. Vincent laughed, and before they knew it, hours had passed.

And then weeks.

Vincent's mom didn't come back until the next month. When she finally did, she immediately disappeared again, and pretty soon, Vincent was living with Francisco almost permanently.

Francisco and Vincent became like brothers, but more than brothers, too, because Viviana's words stuck with Francisco.

He's our responsibility now.

At five years old, Francisco realized he was wrong about a bunch of things: Vincent wasn't imaginary, he wasn't to be feared, and he also wasn't Francisco's guardian angel. In fact, it was the other way around. Vincent was the hardest-luck kid Francisco had ever met in a neighborhood full of hard-luck cases. From then on, for the next eleven years, it would be Francisco who watched over Vincent. Helped him. Played with him. Viviana's words echoing in his ears:

He's our responsibility now.

September 4

Shower. *Check.*

Shave. *Check.*

Pack toothbrush, comb, deodorant. *Check.*

Bags by the door. *Check.*

Francisco looked at the list one more time and crumpled it up. He glanced at his watch. 5:45 A.M. He was ready—ready for the first day of the rest of his life.

Slipping on a button-down shirt, he looked at himself in a small mirror affixed to his wall and pulled a tie around his neck. The duffel went over one shoulder, the backpack over the other. He pulled some dust bunnies off the laces of his shoes, pulled them over his white athletic socks, and tiptoed through the apartment so as not to wake anyone. Passing through the kitchen, he opened the refrigerator and found a big pot of *arroz con pollo*. Francisco folded back the cellophane and ladled out four huge mouthfuls of delicious chicken and rice. It tasted good and spicy as he chewed. A line of juice dribbled out of the corner of his mouth. He wiped it away with the cuff of his shirt, and when he swallowed, he was left with the bittersweet aftertaste of home.

He was gonna miss his mom's cooking. For real. He swung the refrigerator door closed and saw his dad—Ernesto—standing in boxers and a sleeveless ribbed shirt. Ernesto's hair was tangled from sleep, showing more gray hairs than Francisco was used to seeing. His big, firm potbelly poked out naked at the bottom of his shirt.

"Did I wake you?" asked Francisco.

"No. I set my alarm. I wanted to see you before you left."

Francisco nodded and gave a little smile. "I'm going to miss Mom's chicken and rice."

"It's the best I ever tasted. When your mother and I were teenagers in Puerto Rico, she got marriage proposals from all over the island, men who only wanted her *arroz con pollo*."

"How'd you get her to choose you?"

Ernesto thumbed his chest and said with pride, "She likes big talkers." Then he laughed a little and looked shy. Francisco laughed, too. The first pulses of morning light reddened the edges of the window blinds. Standing with his dad in the quiet apartment, looking sharp in a tie and his dad looking old and haggard in his yellowed T-shirt, Francisco was suddenly overcome by sadness.

"Are you proud of me, Pop?"

Emotion filled Ernesto's eyes like he wanted to say a million things. He gave a hard swallow and chose to just embrace his son instead. When he pulled back, his eyes were wet.

"*Study*," he said in a voice that was so choked up that

Francisco could barely hear him. "Study. Work hard. Harder than you've ever worked before."

"I will."

"I mean it, Francisco. Those kids . . . they maybe never even met a Puerto Rican. You have to show them a smart, proud Puerto Rican. Show them a hardworking Puerto Rican. Show them a successful one. Show them what's in your heart." His dad paused to swallow. "I never had the chance to go to school, Francisco. Getting to this country was as much as I could accomplish in my life. It took everything I had to do that, to raise you. So now it's your turn—to take the next step. To make us proud." He patted his son's chest, then stuck out his own chest and patted it. "Show them who *we* are."

Ernesto grabbed Francisco and hugged him one more time, but before Francisco could get his arms around his dad to return the hug, the old man turned away and hurried back to the bedroom. Francisco stood alone in the kitchen. He felt a sense of waiting. The sensation was overpowering. It was as if his apartment—no, all the apartments all across Spanish Harlem—were waiting to see what its golden child would now do. It was time for him to go. Francisco felt the dreams of thousands of sleeping men and women and children waiting for him to realize their dreams, too.

Francisco opened the door. It was the door to the only home he'd ever known, where he'd slept every single night of his life. Then, with just a soft click of the lock to announce his departure, he headed off into the world.

November 8

What in the hell did that crazy fool think he was doing?

Reignbow glared at the teacher. He had these silly "lamb chop" sideburns and thick, black plastic glasses. The sleeves of his plaid flannel shirt were rolled up to his elbows, and his jeans were cuffed above his Converse shoes. Everything about him screamed "Brooklyn hipster."

Oh—and he was white.

Reignbow had never had a white teacher before. What made this worse was the fact that he was teaching her favorite class. Choir. She was the star singer of the class, maybe the best singer in the whole school, but now she was going to have to deal with this guy, and it made her want to quit choir altogether.

This was November, two months into the school year, two months since Francisco left for boarding school. Without him around, nothing in her life felt normal anymore. And now her favorite class had been hijacked by a new kind of strangeness.

Just to be clear, Reignbow didn't have problems with white

people. She wasn't racist or anything (but truth be told, she had friends who were). She believed that everybody had a place in this world. But this guy was clearly out of his element at Alvarez High School.

Reignbow glanced over at her two girlfriends, Dinky and Boondangle. They shared her sneer in a unified showing of utter boredom. Boondangle pulled out a compact and started playing with her hair. Dinky closed her eyes and took a nap. Boonsie and Dink: numbers four and five of the Krew. And these two always came in a pair.

Reignbow stealthily reached into her pocket and opened her cell phone underneath the desk. She had to be careful. Teachers were known for taking cell phones away from kids and never giving them back, although she doubted that this guy had the courage to do that in *this* room. She kept her eyes on the blackboard, pretending to pay attention to the lecture, while her fingers blindly found the keys on her cell phone pad.

F, whr u at? Havnt herd frm u in forver. They got a cell sgnl up there or wht?

She hit Send, closed the phone, and left it cupped inside her hands, waiting, hoping, praying for it to buzz with a response. Reignbow kept on pretending to pay attention to the goofy white boy handing sheets of music around the class, but she heard nothing of what he was saying. Her eyes may have been on the teacher, but her mind was on her phone, and her heart was racing two hundred miles to the north.

Finally, the teacher tapped his hand on a music stand and everyone stood up. "Let's start from the top," he said. Reignbow looked down at the music, opened her mouth, and let free the most beautiful voice any teacher of hers, black, white, green, or orange, had ever heard from a high school student.

11

"Yo, I'm much prettier than *all* these girls," said Dinky, hanging upside down from the monkey bars and flipping through a copy of *Us*. She shook her head pitifully. "These a bunch of nasty celebrities. When is *Us* gonna come to Spanish Harlem and take *my* picture?"

"As soon as they figure out if you're a boy or a girl," said Boondangle.

Dinky flipped over and dismounted from the jungle gym bar, went over to where Boondangle was sitting on a bench, and smacked her with the rolled-up magazine.

"Ow! You messed up my hair!" Boondangle pulled out her compact again and fixed her 'do. Reignbow laughed and turned to look at about a thousand students streaming out the front doors. School was over for the day. The kids were screaming, jumping on each other, running as fast as they could, as if they'd been starved inside that school with no air to breathe.

Dinky and Boondangle were just nicknames. In El Barrio,

even nicknames got nicknames. Dinky also went by D, the Dink, Dinker . . . pretty much anything that started with a *D*. Boondangle went by Boonsie, Boo, and B-dangle . . . which is to say, anything that sounded like a kind of jewelry.

Dinky was the funniest girl Reignbow had ever met. Spry, cute, and nutty, she had a style unto herself. A typical day saw her with fluorescent makeup, a dude's tie (usually polka dotted), and an unwrapped Blow-Pop stuck in her hair to keep it up. She was a star on the girls' basketball team and had this tough, tomboy way of walking.

Boondangle lived farther north and west in a neighborhood that wasn't exactly Spanish Harlem, but wasn't exactly anything else. Boondangle herself was like that, too: not exactly in with the rest of the crowd, pretty but without a strong sense of place in the world, other than in her own heeled shoes. Boondangle was more prissy than the rest of the Krew. She wore too much dangly jewelry and too much makeup (frequently of the bright blue variety). She was reserved like an ice queen, and a real smarty-pants. Kind of annoying but also kind of funny.

"Yo, look at that!" Dinky yelled at Boonsie and Reign. "*Thar she blows!* It's Monika!"

Lost in the sea of students was a large girl with a sloppy black T-shirt stretched over her big front and ratty black sweatpants.

"She's gross," said Boonsie. "When did she get so fat?"

"Yo, don't be so rude. She was pregnant," said Dinky. "Didn't you hear?" They shook their heads. "You kids are out of the loop. She was pregnant five months, and last week, she went to get an abortion."

"What?!" screamed Reignbow and Dinky.

"Yeah. She went to this clinic. I heard all about it. There were a bunch of other girls, all of them waiting for an abortion. The other girls were still little—you know what I mean?—sitting next to their moms or gra'moms. But then there was Monika, sitting by herself with this big belly. Everyone was turning and looking at her belly and getting into her business. They were questioning her and saying, like, 'Why you here? You only have a few more months to go.' They said, 'You're pretty much full term. That's murder!' And then the nurse came, and she thought five months was too late, too, but there was nothing she could do about it except scare Monika. So the nurse brought her into the operating room and showed her all the equipment they were gonna use on her, and said things like they were gonna have to put needles in her stomach. But Monika didn't budge. She crossed her arms and said she was doing it, and that was that, and period. When the nurse asked her why, you know what her excuse was?"

"What?"

"That she don't like her boyfriend. And her mother was ready to support her and everything."

"That's awful!" yelled Boondangle.

"That is some shit," said Reignbow.

Dinky went on. "Monika said, 'I don't like my boyfriend nomore. He's retarded.' Five months pregnant!"

Boondangle shook her head. "Abortion is a sin, and that girl is going to hell." Then she passed her lip balm to Dinky. "Take this. Your lips are dry. You look scary."

Dinky rubbed the balm into her lips.

"It just goes to show," said Boondangle, "why you shouldn't mess around with boys this young. Boys suck."

Dinky snorted. "They don't suck."

"Yeah, they do."

"Stop lying. *You* suck, that's why."

Boondangle laughed and waved her off. "In fact, I'm extremely cool."

"I think it depends on the guy," Reignbow said.

Boondangle groaned, unconvinced. "Personally, I think they all suck."

"Please," said Dinky. "My father, he talks to me about boys. He teaches me the basics of, like, 'Don't let no dude disrespect you or take advantage of you.' Then I'm, like, 'It ain't gonna happen.' Because I'll fight dudes, you know? I watch Lifetime, all right? So if you come at me, I'm gonna come at you!"

Boondangle burst into giggles. But Dinky was serious. "You know, I tried to do that situation: have a little boyfriend. One time, I met this boy, and I be, like, 'You gonna take me out, *pappi*?'"

Reign and Boondangle laughed.

"No, look! Listen to my story! You gonna take me out, *pappi*? He was like, '*Sí, mamacita*.' I think he's going to take me out to some place like Mama Mexico——"

"Or Uno's——"

"Yeah!"

Boondangle nodded. "Or Primavera."

Dinky groaned. "Mmm! Primavera's seriously good, you dig? So I'm thinking he's going to take me to someplace like that. But you know where he takes me? He takes me to *Mc-Donald's*."

Her two friends screamed with laughter, but Dinky was furious talking about it. "I said, 'I don't want to go to McDonald's.' So he says he's gonna take me to the . . . um . . . *cuchifrito*."

"Nooo!"

"The food truck on the corner?"

"That's why you should wait until you're older to start a relationship," Reignbow said.

"Reign. Why d'you hafta come at me like that? You ain't so much older than me. You're lucky to be in love and all that shit."

"Shit! What shit?"

"You know, all cheesy."

"I'm not cheesy!"

"Yes you are! You get around Francisco and you start blushing. You be, like, 'Oh my gosh, Francisco! You're the best thing that's ever happened to me!' " Dinky pumped her hand under her shirt like a heartbeat. "And your heart is going like this! Boom! Boom! Boom!"

Reignbow laughed. "No way! It's not like that at all! It's just, I've never felt this strongly for a guy. We're probably gonna be together forever. I know it."

"You do?" asked Boondangle.

"Yeah."

"For*ever*?"

"Of course."

"But how exactly is it going to work out with him gone and everything? Like, have you thought about that?"

"We've talked about it, actually. You know, it's been pretty much the highlight of every conversation we've had lately. We've talked about if I was to move away, or if he was to move away, that we would stay together. You know? Like, especially if one of us has more . . . or a better—"

Boondangle butted in, all smarty-pants: "*Opportunity.* That's what you're trying to say."

"Uh-huh."

"But then is he, like, going to come back down after he graduates? Because there's no way you can leave Spanish Harlem with your mom sick and everything."

"Well—"

"Or are you saying that he'd do college in the city? But then that really narrows his choices, you know?"

"Well . . . I don't know . . . in *exact* terms. We'll have to see. All I know is that after we both graduate from high school, I can see myself marrying him."

"Holy shit," squealed the Dink, slack-jawed. "Reign, go wash your mouth with soap right now!"

"I just don't see how that's going to happen," said Boondangle.

"Yo," said Reign, "Boon. Why you hatin' on me?"

"I'm not hatin'. I'm just being realistic. Long-distance relationships never work. They always start out good, with everyone promising to stay in touch and visit. But then a couple weeks go by, and you forget to call, or he forgets to call, and the whole relationship just fizzles."

Silence. Dink turned her head to Reignbow.

"Well?" said Dinky, "What's up with that? Has Fran been in touch with you?"

"Yeah," stammered Reignbow, as if her words were coming from someone else's mouth. "Today, actually."

"Today?" said Boonsie, clearly skeptical.

"Yes. Today. He wrote me the most amazing text. And, in case you wanted to know, he was also in touch with me yesterday. Twice yesterday. We talked in the morning, and then at night before I went to bed. He put me to sleep on the phone. It was so romantic."

Dink shrugged. "That's good enough for me. Case closed. You guys gonna be married and shit. Babies within two years. I know it." Boondangle shook her head skeptically. Dinky ignored her and asked, "So how's he doing at school, anyway? Does he like it up there?"

"Yeah, uh, he's doing great. He's, like, one of the smartest kids at that school. Getting straight A's." Reignbow smiled, lying through her teeth.

Dinky whistled, impressed. "Wow. It's really going to happen for him, huh? He's going to go to some great college. Harvard, or some shit, and become a big deal. Maybe even president. Our first Hispanic president!"

Reignbow laughed nervously. "Anyway, I gotta go. Mom needs me." She hauled off down the street. It was an odd departure, fast, and Boonsie picked up on it. She could tell something was up, but she had no idea what—and she wasn't going to say anything, at least not until she had some facts on the situation.

12

"Reign! You're late! We're already supposed to be at the bank by now!"

"I *know*, Mom. Stop nagging me."

Reignbow slammed the door behind her. She went to the kitchen to grab an apple. She'd had enough problems today, and she did *not* want any more grief—especially from her mom.

"The bank closes in twenty minutes. Where have you been?"

"With my friends. Hanging out. Like every other kid in the world. It's only me who has to come home early for junk."

"It's not junk, honey. It's responsi*bility*. We all have responsibilities. Today is one of yours."

"Dinky and Boonsie don't have responsibilities."

"Exactly. And all they do is gossip and do nothing with their lives. That will lead them nowhere."

Reignbow rolled her eyes. Of all her mom's attitudes— "tough love" mom, "strict" mom, "trying to be funny" mom— "inspirational" mom was the least tolerable.

Reignbow bit into the apple and looked inside. It was rotten. She scrunched up her face and spit it into the trash.

"I'm hungry, Lily," said Reignbow, using her mom's first name to annoy her.

Lily wheeled herself to the coatrack, grabbing her parka. Reignbow noticed she was using the hand-crank wheelchair.

"Aren't we taking the electric?"

"Battery's been acting up. You're going to have to push."

"But it's like a mile, Mom. I'm gonna have to run the whole way!"

"Then you better stop wasting time."

Reignbow stepped behind the wheelchair, took hold of the cracked plastic handles, and shoved her mom out the front door. Lily gripped the armrests to keep from bouncing out.

"That was a little hard, honey."

"Do you want to get there or not?"

Lily didn't respond. She wasn't one to complain. The bulk of her problems started ten years ago, back when she was a single mom on welfare with two kids—Reignbow, who was six at the time, and an older daughter, Jesenia, who was eleven. It was a cold, rainy winter day. Lily and the little girls had been grocery shopping, carrying about a hundred bags down into the subway. The three of them were soaked to the bone, miserable, shivering, and carrying those wet grocery bags. They squished into their seats on the crowded train. Little Reignbow cried with hunger. Lily had three slices of pizza, cold and wet, balanced between the bags. She handed a slice to each child and told them to pray over their meal.

A few people in the subway car turned to watch. It was

quite a sight——a show of strength, dignity. This cold little family praying over their cold, wet pizzas. Lily prayed the hardest, harder than she'd prayed in years. When she finished her prayer, Lily looked up and said "amen," and saw an ad posted above the doors.

GET YOUR DEGREE AT DEXTER COLLEGE
Our students are mothers, fathers, full-time
workers, old, young, and poor.
What's *your* excuse?

Well, Lily couldn't think of an excuse. She wrote down the phone number on one of her bags. A year later, Lily had an associate's degree. A few months after that, she had a job in a Bronx hospital as a medical records technician. Even though so many other families from her neighborhood were struggling on welfare, broke, selling drugs here and there, Lily was employed. With a proper job.

It was a miracle. The answer to her prayers.

Until it wasn't.

Just three years later, Lily's career was over. She got sick. *Mad* sick. Her legs gave out one day, and she couldn't walk anymore. Then she went blind in one eye. She started to age really, really fast. She went to a bunch of doctors, had about a million tests done, until they finally diagnosed her with a disease that took Lily a full day just to learn how to pronounce: multiple sclerosis.

It was the end of her career. And the end of life as she knew it.

Now, MS isn't like most diseases. MS is a sort of gumball machine of lots of different symptoms. Put your quarter in, and everyone gets a different problem, a differently colored gumball. For some people, it makes their hands go numb. For other people, it ruins their eyesight. But for the really unlucky folks, they get a whole assortment of problems. All the gumballs come flying out of the machine at once. And that's pretty much what happened to Lily.

Hobbled, infirm, halfway blind, it made her wonder why God would answer her prayer on that wet, rainy day on the subway, only to take it away.

Her wheelchair bumped and jostled through the crowds rushing past her. Reignbow dodged a big hole in the sidewalk, making her way as fast as she could along 110th Street, all the way over to the West Side of Manhattan.

"You know, we got banks in Spanish Harlem, too," said Reignbow, huffing and puffing. "We don't need to be going this far."

"I don't trust 'em," said Lily. "When I was a kid, banks refused to even be in our 'hood. Wasn't a branch for a mile. Now, there's banks all over the place, but they're just looking to take advantage of the poor."

"You're being paranoid, Ma."

Lily turned around as best she could to face Reignbow. "You should pay more attention in school, Reign. Banks have always had a messed-up relationship with poor neighborhoods. Either they ignore us or they're digging shoulder-deep into our pockets. And those check-cashing joints are worse. Fifteen percent fees! How's anyone supposed to make a living when a dollar everywhere else is worth just eighty-five cents in the 'hood?" Lily made a disapproving *tsk*. "I'm boycotting the whole thing."

"Easy for you to say. You don't have to push this wheel-chair."

"Well, at least the West Side ain't got none of that history, Reign. All the nickel-and-diming that the banks do over there is the normal sort of ripping off they'd do for anyone, minority *or* white."

Reignbow didn't have the breath to challenge her mom anymore, so she just rolled her eyes and shoved onward.

13

$2,176.03. That was the amount of the check that Lily had folded up in the front pocket of her purse. That was the amount she got every month in disability payments ever since the year that MS short-circuited her body and blew the fuse on her career—$2,176.03 per month. Not a lot. But not too bad, either. After she wrote out a $935 check to cover rent, Lily went to the bank and cashed the monthly payment.

Now, the monthly trips to the bank weren't all bad. Not as far as Reignbow saw it. There was good stuff, too. The Upper West Side was like being in another country for her. She loved to look in the windows of trendy restaurants and expensive clothes shops like Gap and American Apparel. It was a weird reminder that not everyone saw New York as a place to struggle. Some people saw the city as a playground. A place to spend money and not feverishly hoard it.

Reignbow daydreamed about shopping on the Upper West

Side, eating there, having dates with Francisco there, all kinds of sweet things.

When Lily was done at the bank, and had her $2,176.03 minus $935 in cash, they turned around to go back to Spanish Harlem.

Lily's cash would last them a month: groceries that food stamps didn't cover, cable bill, water bill, every other kind of bill. Whatever money was left over, even if it was just a few dollars, Lily put away in a box in her bedroom closet. She called it her "rainy day" box and decorated it with storm clouds and rain. Behind the clouds, she drew a rainbow.

The amazing thing, though, was that for a woman in Lily's circumstances, she hadn't ever had to dip into the box. Maybe it was her stinginess, or maybe it was her optimism that helped her survive, because it takes quite a woman to live through such storms in life and not once see any of them as a rainy day.

14

A piece of steak spattered in a puddle of oil. Reignbow used a fork to jab at the gristly slab a few times. She couldn't get today's trip to the bank out of her head. She wanted to move there. Leave the 'hood. Live somewhere else, like the Upper West Side. Or maybe somewhere farther, beyond New York . . . another city perhaps. Another state. Maybe even a small town. Reignbow was sixteen, smart, and not pregnant. A talented singer. She could go anywhere. Do anything. Didn't she have hopes and dreams, too?

Frustrated, she jabbed the steak and slapped it over, splattering hot oil on her arm. A dull red patch emerged. She scratched at it a few times, then dragged the meat onto a plate.

"Mom! Steak's ready!" Reignbow yelled, wincing at the stuttering whir from Lily's wheelchair. It was the loneliest sound Reignbow ever heard. This apartment used to be full of voices, laughter, life. That was back when Reignbow's older sister lived there, before she moved out, never to be heard from again. And

Francisco used to be over all the time, too. But now it was just Reignbow and Lily. Two of them, left behind to hold down this crumbling fort. To rot, while others traveled on for brighter horizons.

After dinner, Reignbow drew a bath. She wheeled her mother into the bathroom and helped remove her clothes. There were suction-cupped handles installed in the bathroom, and Lily grabbed them with shaking arms as Reignbow lowered her into the steaming hot water.

A half hour later, Lily called for Reignbow to help her out of the bath again. Reignbow got her mother's robe for her and helped her into bed. Reignbow kissed her mother on the forehead, turned out the light, and closed the door.

That night, Reignbow had a dream. A nightmare, actually. She dreamt that she was in the forest. Francisco was with her, but he was playing games on her—he kept hiding behind trees, laughing, darting from tree to tree to stay ahead of her grasp. *F! F! Come back!* she kept yelling, but he wouldn't stop playing. She wanted to reach out and grab him, hold him, hug him. Be with him. But Francisco didn't answer her, and the game turned violent and strange. Whenever Francisco got behind a tree, he'd shove the tree down at Reignbow.

Francisco! she cried in her dream. *Stop! You're going to kill me!*

But Francisco kept laughing, leaping from tree to tree and shoving them down on her, tree to tree to tree. Reignbow was running to stay clear of the collapsing behemoths, begging for him to stop, as he made one final push and sent the entire forest crashing down on her—

Bzzzz!

Reignbow jumped out of bed, gasping for air.

Bzzzz! Bzzzz!

Morning sunlight, thin and yellow, brightened through her window. There was a gentle knocking on her bedroom door. It was Lily.

"Reign? Reign, honey? You awake? You're going to be late for school."

"Just a second, Mom!"

Reignbow pushed a clump of sweaty hair out of her face and grabbed the buzzing cell phone off her dresser. Gasping, she opened the phone and saw a small envelope-shaped icon on the screen. Reignbow clicked to open.

In hood 2nite. shrt but sweet. F.

"Oh my God!"

Reignbow closed the phone and pressed it to her heart. She wanted to scream. Reignbow opened her phone and typed a message back.

happiest girl in wrld rite now aftr WRST nite. cant wait to see u!

15

November 9

All the clothes that were supposed to be in her closet were lying on the floor. Reignbow stood over the heap like a sculptor whose masterpiece had collapsed into a chaotic mess.

"I have nothing to wear, Ma!"

There was no answer from Lily.

"Ma-a-a-a!!!"

It was enough to make her scream. She'd spent the whole day at school thinking about Francisco. Excitement filled her chest while nervousness gutted her stomach. She wanted tonight to be perfect. During chemistry class, she matched tops and accessories into killer outfits in her head while the other students matched atoms of hydrogen and carbon into ethylene. But, when school ended and she rushed home, everything that looked great in her imagination failed to go together.

"Ma! I need you!"

Lily wheeled herself into Reignbow's room. "What's wrong?"

"Look." She kicked through the clothes like they were a pile of leaves. "Can you find one thing that's gonna wow Francisco?"

"Well, sure."

"Okay, what?"

"All of it. The same things you wowed him with when you saw him every day two months ago." She patted Reignbow's cheek reassuringly. "It hasn't been that long, honey. You act like he's been off at war or something."

Reignbow put her hands on her hips and gave her mother a stern glare. "You don't get it."

"Oh, I get it." She winked.

"No, you don't. And even if you do, I'm gonna pretend you don't."

Lily laughed out loud. "I was young, too, Reign."

"I don't want to hear it!" yelled Reignbow, covering her ears.

Bang bang bang. Someone was at the door. Reignbow grabbed her mom in desperation.

"That's him! You answer it while I figure something out."

Lily sighed and wheeled down the hallway, while Reignbow slammed her bedroom door shut.

The first thing that struck him were the smells. Roasted vegetables, Spanish rice. Chinese takeout. It intermingled with the faint odor of pee and bleach. And then there were the sounds: salsa music from one apartment door, hip-hop from another. There was the sharp laughter of boys play-fighting, girls yammering, echoing and mixing together.

Francisco took it all in. He was *home.* And he had missed it.

Crazy as that might seem, he'd missed it all so much. He stood in the twenty-fourth-floor corridor with a casual, preppy slouch that was new for him. Something he'd picked up at school. Realizing how he was standing, he shifted his weight and pulled his pants lower across his butt.

Francisco had been in Spanish Harlem for all of twenty minutes, and he couldn't wait to see everyone. He was at his apartment for only a few seconds—just enough time to drop off his bags, hug his surprised parents, dry his mom's tears, and promise to be back for dinner—before running off to Reignbow's building.

"Yo, Reignbow! You home?" he yelled through the metal door. The door, always slightly tilted on its hinges, wrenched open. Lily's face brightened, and her arms flew up for a hug.

"How *are* you?" she said into his shoulder. "It's so good to see you."

"I'm good, I'm good," he said, underplaying his excitement.

"Stand back, let me see you. Look how handsome you are!"

He grinned and blushed. "Is Reign around?"

"Reignbow!" yelled Lily.

"Coming!"

"Your Francisco is here!" she called. "Well, you're *our* Francisco."

Francisco shifted uncomfortably. From down the hall, several other deadbolts chunked and cranked, and doors opened. Five or six neighbors poked their heads out. When they saw Francisco, they pushed out their hands for shakes and hugs.

"Welcome home, big shot!"

"It's the whiz kid! Good to be back?"

"*Great* to be back," Francisco said.

"How's the team up there, champ?" asked one old man, Mr. Gonzalez, whom Francisco had known since he was a kid.

"Not bad," said Francisco. "But we got a lot of work to do."

"I'm surprised they even know what basketball is."

"They play like those old black-and-white clips where everyone just stands in place and passes the ball around."

Everyone laughed. Francisco kept looking past Lily for Reignbow. He was more nervous than he'd expected.

"You got so strong and handsome up at that school!" said a middle-aged grandmother who stood at a door farther down the hall. "What're they feeding you up there?"

"Nothing good. Food's so bad everyone looks trim." More laughter. "Reign's home, right?" he asked Lily again.

"She's getting dressed."

"Oh, you haven't seen your girl yet!" squealed a woman in her eighties, wearing a flower-print housedress. "This is going to be so romantic!" She took a long drag off her menthol cigarette and settled into the doorway to watch. Others concurred.

Francisco shook his head. "Y'all got to get out of here," he said. But then a voice pulled his attention away.

"Fran?"

He turned and saw Reignbow standing in the doorway. Pink shirt. Jeans. Simple and beautiful, always her best style.

"Hey," he said quietly.

"Hey."

They sort of froze there, looking at each other. Reignbow

heard throat clearing down the hall from the audience that had assembled.

"What's going on?" she whispered to Francisco.

"Kiss her!" blurted out the old woman with the cigarette.

"That's it," said Francisco. "You all gotta go!" He ran down the hall and shut the doors one by one. "Sorry, everyone." He came back to Reign and gently closed the door on Lily, as well. "Sorry, Ms. Rivera," he said.

Then, with this brief pause of privacy, Francisco took Reignbow at the waist and pulled her in, kissing her deeply. Tugging, touching, she lost herself in his kiss.

In that moment, Francisco found himself. After two months away in a strange place surrounded by strange people, he'd returned to the place he loved, to the girl he loved. With his eyes closed, two months of bizarre and stressful experiences faded away—experiences he'd promised himself that he wouldn't tell to a single soul—and he was just Francisco again. Francisco from the 'hood. Francisco with his girl.

Down the hall, the eighty-something woman with the cigarette cracked her door open again to watch. It was a long kiss, never-ending. The old woman smiled and waved her fingers in front of her face, cooling herself off, and then silently closed her door.

16

"I feel like I haven't seen you in years," said Reignbow. She led him by the hand through Hope Park, stopping him at the bridge and kissing him. "Why does it feel so long?"

"I don't know. But I know what you mean." He slung his arms around her shoulders and pulled her in tight.

Francisco was unlike all her former boyfriends. Other boys used to hold her like she was an umbrella. Stiff and away. Boys usually held girls in one of two ways: either like they wanted to screw them or like they were feeling obligated to be nice to them. But Francisco held Reignbow with the weight in his body, pressing himself like he needed her—like he needed her love. His body felt strong to her, but his need felt even stronger.

"So this is all I get? A few hours' notice that you're coming home?" she said, lightly pounding on his chest, pretending to be mad. "I didn't have time to plan anything."

"I don't want anything. I just want you."

"All right—so what are you doing here?"

"School break."

"Already?"

Francisco tossed his thumb over his shoulder. "You want me to go back?"

"No, no!" She devoured his hands with her hands. "Stay."

"It's Veterans Day weekend. You get it off, too."

"Yeah, but I kind of imagined you chained to your desk up there, the teachers whipping you to study more. I didn't think they'd let you out so soon."

"Well, we're so smart that we can actually study less than you guys and still learn twice as much."

"Don't say that." She whacked him. "It's the reason I told myself for why you never e-mailed—that you were too busy."

"Well, I didn't get any calls, either. No letters."

"I know. It's because you came back too early. They're on my bed. You can read them when you come over."

"I'd like that," he said, locking eyes with her. In the past, they could do this forever, just hold each other's gaze. Read each other's thoughts.

"You look different," she finally said.

"I do?"

"Yeah."

"How do I look different?"

"I don't know. Just different."

Francisco raised his nose and talked like a white person. "More educated? More proper?"

"Nooooo!" She laughed. "I can't figure it out exactly. Just something . . ." She looked him up and down. "I'll figure out your secrets."

"That's fine. Let me know when you know, okay?"

"I will."

He touched a strand of the hair hanging long over her shoulder. "You've changed. Your hair color's different."

"Yeah. And I got fat, too." She made a disappointed face.

"You haven't got fat."

"Yes I did."

"No you haven't."

She sighed at the compliment.

"Maybe you got a little thick around the thighs, but not fat. . . ." He laughed.

"Shut up!" she said. "Take it back."

"I take it back."

"Good. So tell me, big shot who hasn't changed at all, how is it up at that school?"

He hesitated at first. "Reignbow, I gotta tell you . . ."

"What?"

"That school is the best thing that ever happened to me."

"Yeah?"

"You can't believe what it's like. The teachers are actually interesting, you know? They're not just standing there reading out of a book like our teachers did—they actually know what they're teaching. Oh, and there's kids from all over. From China, Africa, France. From places I never even heard of."

"So you gonna remember us when you get big?"

He laughed.

"Just remember, *this* is your home. I don't know nothing about people from China. But I know Spanish Harlem. And I know you. No matter what happens, who you meet, where you go, this is where you belong." She took his hand and put it on her cheek. "And this is who you belong to. All right?"

"All right."

"You're missed here. We miss you more down here than they miss you up there, I promise."

"I know."

"So you seen the Krew yet?"

"Nope. Came to see you first."

"That's my man. So when do you have to go back?"

"Monday night. I got the long weekend."

"Good. 'Cause, see, I kinda fibbed. I did make *one* plan for us. There's a street festival tonight, up on One Sixteenth. I think the whole Krew's gonna be there, because it's the last one before winter. If you came, it would be like old times again."

"I'd like that a lot."

"So it's a date?"

"It's a date," he said, smiling, but a bit wearily.

As they walked out of the park, she realized what was different about him. He was tired. She'd never seen him so exhausted, and she'd never seen him trying to act happy when he wasn't. Reignbow pulled him in tight. As long as she had him close like this, whatever was going on with him, she knew she could fix everything.

17

While Francisco was with Reignbow, Vincent was thirty blocks north, up in Black Harlem, playing hoops with his man Jason. That would be Jason "J-Dog" Jackson: the sixth and last member of the Krew.

Jason was a black kid, like Vincent. Both of them were part of the Krew, but they had different roots than Reign, Francisco, Boondangle, and Dinky. Vincent and Jason definitely had their own kind of friendship going on.

Jason was a pretty good baller, even though he was a big kid. A seriously big boy. Jason got no air when he jumped, so he played a faraway game, from the foul line, blasting perimeter shots like howitzers. He wore hoodies and jeans every single day. Come winter, come summer, rain or shine, those same hoodies and those same jeans.

He and Vincent were playing a two-man game; Jason held the brick between his hands. The score was tied. Jason moved for the hoop. Vincent slapped at the brick but got more of Jason than the ball and sent the fat boy sprawling to the ground. Vincent grabbed the ball and went in for an easy layup.

"Foul!" yelled Jason.

"That wasn't no foul. You tripped."

"Yo," said Jason, slowly getting up and rubbing his shoulder. "That was full-on assault and battery."

"Then you shouldn't get in my way, fatso."

"I gotta take a TO."

Jason winced and tucked the ball under his butt, sitting down. He stretched out the pain while Vincent stood there lonesome in the cold wind, looking off, mad and distracted.

"What's your problem?" said Jason.

"*Nuthin'.*"

Jason shrugged. The pain was starting to feel better. "Hey, did you hear that Francisco is back?"

"Yeah. I heard he's back. So what?"

"So *what*?"

"So. What. I mean, look around, Jason. Fran's back, but is he over here with us?" Vincent shook his head, answering his own question. "Nope."

"Oh, so that's what's going on with you."

"Like I already said, ain't nothin' goin' on."

"It's not a big deal, V. He had to go see his girl. He misses her."

"What about his boys, man! Damn." Vincent grabbed the ball from under Jason and set up for a shot. "What d'you think? You think girls the only ones who got feelings?"

"Are you serious?"

"Yeah!"

"You know what, V, you're kinda sounding like a bitch right now."

"I'm sounding like a *bitch*, nigga?"

Jason laughed. "Yeah, you're sounding like a bitch. Come on. Throw me the brick. We *boys*."

"What d'you mean, I'm sounding like a bitch?"

Jason jumped up and grabbed for the ball. Vincent fought him off. Jason taunted him, "We *boys*. C'mon!"

Vincent held the ball tight and stood his ground. "Get the hell outta here, Jase. Listen to me: I told him. I warned that dude. I said, 'You gonna change up there, yo. You gonna be different when you come back.' And you know what? He is. I'm like a goddamn fortune-teller. He don't care about his boys nomore. All he cares about is getting it on with his girl, gettin' a quick piece of her and then goin' back to school. But pretty soon, he won't even be comin' back for her, either. It's all over for him." Vincent shook his head. Sadness enveloped him. He missed his best friend, simple fact. He threw a fist through the air to pretend that his sadness was anger. "But like I said, I really don't care, man."

"I don't know. I think you're being too sensitive about the situation."

"Man, I ain't bein' sensitive! You don't understand! Since we was kids, we used to roll together. Now he be Mr. Upstate . . . boarding-school . . . tie-wearing . . . khaki-pants motherfucker. I mean, we did mad shit together."

"Wait, wait. Are you saying that if you had the same opportunity to go to a better school, you wouldn't take it?"

Vincent laughed. "Ha! Well, I didn't get the opportunity,

did I? What're you talking about? Come on, man. He could've stayed in school down here. What's the difference? They got the same shit. They teach the same shit."

Jason leered. "Oh, yeah? So you think up there they got metal detectors at their school, too?"

"The point is, he's missing everything *we* got to offer."

Jason lifted his finger toward a man pushing a shopping cart full of cans. "Like that guy? I don't know. I think I'd rather be at boarding school."

"Then go. Harlem's got it *all*, baby. The whole world is here. The best recording stars come out of here. Listen, Jase, me and you need to start making some tracks. Okay? Me and you'll start making some real paper. You dig, Jason?"

"I dig. I dig, I guess."

"Good." Vincent drove the basketball hard past Jason, who stood back rigidly, watching his friend, hearing his words, but not understanding him. Vincent scored by himself and threw his arms up in a big, showy victory. "Take *that* with you to boarding school, nigga!"

Jason shook his head. "Yo, I gotta go."

"Then go." Vincent drove to the hoop again and scored one more time. He yelled to Jason, "That's twenty-one. I just beat your ass!"

But Jason was already off the court.

"Quitter!" yelled Vincent.

"Whatever!" Jason screamed. "When I see you tonight, you better not be acting this way."

"What's tonight?"

"Street carnival!"

Vincent nodded.

"One Sixteenth. Everyone going. Maybe even Fran."

"Then *maybe* I'll be there. Maybe I'll come just to talk some sense into our dude." Vincent scratched his head and then remembered. "Yo, Jase, I'm sorry I bumped you, ai'ight?"

"Ai'ight."

"You need any aspirin or anything?" He pointed to his building a few blocks away. "I got aspirin up there."

"No, I'm good."

"You sure?"

"Shut up already. I'm fine."

"Ai'ight. Then I'll see you tonight. For real."

Jason disappeared around the corner, still rubbing his sore shoulder.

18

The sun was down, but the sky was turning bright with colors, illuminated by the strobing lights of a dozen spinning rides. Thousands of people filled the streets with glow sticks and flashing hats. Francisco and Reignbow passed through a corral of blue barricades and a handful of cops playing on their cell phones. Francisco clutched Reignbow's hand so that she wouldn't get lost in the crowds. Sparklers and miniature Puerto Rican flags waved in their faces. Reignbow looked up at the rides that streaked neon flames across the sky. The Ferris wheel, the Scrambler, the Zipper, the Gravitron.

"Where the Krew gonna be?" Francisco yelled to Reign above the din of voices and music and laughter.

"The Zipper!"

Francisco seemed to know everyone. And everyone seemed to know that he was back in the 'hood. He got handshakes and congratulations thrown at him wherever he went.

There was Mr. Herrera, Francisco's old science teacher, with his wife and three children. The teacher gave Francisco a big hug. Mr. Herrera said something in Francisco's ear, but Francisco couldn't hear him above the noise.

"What'd you say?"

"I *said* that it's *students* like *you* who are the *reason* I *teach*!"

Reignbow rubbed Francisco's back, unabashedly proud, and they moved on through the crowd. A hand stuck out and tapped Francisco on the chest. A group of potheads pulled around him and Reignbow. They'd seen these guys before, big-time pot smokers from Alvarez High School, but they weren't like most pot smokers. They weren't mellow. Weren't cool. They were mean little pricks, each one of them, grinning at Francisco with mischievous little mouths twitching out their *hello*s and *hey*s and *whatsup*s.

"I'm good, I'm good. How's things with you guys?" said Francisco. Calm. Collected.

"Not as good as you, fancy pants." A few of them laughed.

"I get it," said Francisco. "I get it. Fancy pants. Just let us through, ai'ight?"

Nobody moved. "So, you're, like, a sellout, right?" said one kid.

"Chill, chill," said Francisco. "Who's selling anything? I'm not buying. I'm just having a night out with my girl."

"Go fuck yourself all the way back to school," said another.

"I'll be sure to do that," said Francisco. He gently pushed himself through the cluster of boys. A few shoved middle fingers in his face, but they let him go.

Reignbow pulled in closer to Francisco and sighed with

relief. She saw her girlfriends ahead of them and pointed to the Zipper ride, which was tossing its small cages full of people high into the sky and then swooping them back down fast and dangerously close to the ground. Boonsie and Dink watched the ride while slurping frosty drinks through curlicue straws. Dink was wearing glow sticks in her hair.

"Ohmygodit'sFrancisco!" shouted Dinky, and she rushed at him with a hug that sent him flying back a few steps.

"Good to see you, too, crazy," said Francisco. Boonsie sauntered over, and they all started talking a million miles an hour. "Where Vincent at?" asked Francisco.

"Boo!" someone screamed behind them, and Vincent and then Jason leapt out from the crowd and piled into the conversation. Vincent and Francisco hugged and slapped their hands together.

"Welcome back, Fran!"

"Yo, it's good to be back. Good to be here."

"Hey, guys! Check this out!" said Jason. He reached into his pocket and pulled out a long row of ride tickets. "I found 'em on the ground." Everyone grabbed at the tickets. Reignbow was distracted, looking around at the lights, soaking in the night.

In nearby apartment buildings, she saw old people in pajamas leaning out of their windows, smoking cigarettes and watching the fair. They looked bored by everyone else's fun. The smell of sausages and peppers warmed the air. Vendors nestled into every nook of available space, selling CDs and stolen movies, wind-up toys, live lizards climbing inside mason jars, packs of batteries. One guy was selling knives with carved wooden handles. Young, dangerous-looking teens were checking them out. The rides glided in and out of the sky like hovercrafts from a science-fiction movie, landing and letting kids stagger out, dizzy and elated. With tickets in hand, the Krew got into line for the Ferris wheel.

Dink and Reignbow got into one car together. Boondangle got into another car by herself, saying she wanted to enjoy the view in peace and quiet without everyone's yammering. The boys opted to stay down on the ground and just watch, because they said they wanted to catch up—but Reignbow suspected that they were just scared to go up so high. The Ferris wheel started with a jolt. Reign and Dinky soared over the upper reaches of East Harlem. They were up higher than anything else in the neighborhood, trees, billboards—except for the housing projects. Nothing was bigger than the projects.

The Ferris wheel shook in the wind. Reign grabbed Dinky for dear life.

"You *scared*?" Dinky laughed. "You scared of this baby ride!"

"This ain't no baby ride."

"Just wait till the Gravitron. That shit's *fast*."

Reignbow could see the moon clearly from up there. "Look! Look how big it is!"

"That's what *she* said," said Dinky, giggling. It took Reignbow a second to get the joke.

"Why're you always talking about sex?" said Reignbow.

" 'Cause if I don't, no one else will."

"Hey! I talk about sex."

"No you don't."

"Yes I do."

"No you don't. Face it, Reign, you're just not a horny girl."

"And how would you know?"

"Answer me this: F's gone for two months. You've had, like, four hours with him. How many times you guys done it so far?"

"Shut up!"

"I would have done him at least three by now."

"Now, that sounds weird. I don't want you thinking about my man having sex."

"That ain't what I meant. I'm just saying, it's 'cause you're in love—now you guys are all serious and shit."

"Love?"

"Yeah. You're in love. True love."

Reignbow smiled and turned the thought over in her head like a diamond, looking at every side of it. She liked thinking this way. Feeling this way. It made her feel strong and new. "So what? I guess it is love. I mean, whatever it is, it's something big."

"That's what *I* said," screamed Dinky. This time, Reignbow laughed right away.

Then the Ferris wheel churned toward the ground. Dinky leaned way out of the car and called out to Jason, Vincent, and Francisco.

"Lame-ass chicken shits!"

They gave her the finger. As the car swept along the bottom, Jason unleashed a howl and ran at the Ferris wheel. He jumped past a whole crowd of kids waiting in line, hopped a fence, and—in an amazing feat of agility for such a big kid—leapt into the Ferris wheel car with the girls. It went rocking like crazy, like the whole thing was going to snap off. The guy who operated the ride screamed bloody murder at Jason, but it was too late to stop him. Reignbow, Dink, and Jason went shooting up into the sky, laughing and shoving each other to make more room.

Reignbow glowed. What a night. She thought that one day, they'd count Spanish Harlem among the great civilizations of the world that she'd learned about at school, like Greece, Egypt, and Rome. No place was happier than Spanish Harlem. Brighter. More fun. No friends were better than hers. And in the history of the world, no one had loved like Reignbow loved Francisco. Their story, she thought, would be one for the ages.

The night ended suddenly, like someone pulled the plug. Hundreds of neon lights flickered and then turned off. The faces of the Krew, lit red and green and purple, fell into darkness. Those depressing, gray-slabbed housing projects they'd forgotten about for a couple hours seemed to return, as if dinosaurs long extinct once again dominated the skyline. Dinky and Boons headed off together, down the street, waving to their friends, going to their respective homes. Reignbow yawned and wanted to go home, too. But Vincent was all hyped up, acting crazy like he could have gone all night.

"Yo, Fran, I know about a party up in my 'hood. Come on up."

"No, no. It's late, bro. I gotta get home."

"What for? Yo, this party could be *good*."

"Yeah? Whose party?"

"You don't know this cat. I met him after you left. But it's gonna be *dope*."

"Yeah?" said Francisco, sounding a little excited.

"F," interrupted Reignbow, "I'm tired, you know?"

"Yeah, yeah," said Francisco, feeling pulled in two directions. "Maybe next time, V."

"Why? She can walk herself home. She does it when you're not around."

"Yeah, but he *is* around tonight," shot back Reignbow.

"Chill, chill everyone," said Francisco. "Vincent, I'm gonna walk Reignbow home. But I had fun with you, V. It was like old times."

"What fun you talkin' about? Me and you barely even said anything. Barely hung out."

"Let's hang out tomorrow. Chill. It's all good."

Vincent shook his head and glared off into the streets. "Yeah. Whatever."

"Not whatever. Seriously."

"Naw, don't promise me nothing, dawg, because tomorrow this party'll be over."

"Believe me. Go to your party. Have fun. Stay out of trouble. Get some sleep, and I'll see you tomorrow."

"Yo, believe *me*: Drop your girl off and *then* meet me at the party."

"Why you pushing this, Vin? I can't. I'm gonna drop Reignbow off and then I gotta be up early in the morning to study."

"Study? Seriously? But you only home for a weekend."

"They don't care."

"They make you study when you're home?"

"I guess."

There was an uncomfortable pause between the two old friends.

"All right," said Vincent. "I'll tune in tomorrow. Listen for your next excuse then."

"Quit that, V." Francisco wrapped his arms around Vincent and gave him a generous hug. "Take care of yourself tonight. You'll be seeing my ass tomorrow. I swear."

Vincent headed off into the night, a lone soul lit in the neon glare of liquor stores. Vincent never walked a straight line. He jagged left, right, looking everywhere: into cars, into trash cans. He dug for coins in pay phones. His eyes and fingers got into everything on the street; he was a scavenger. A survivor. Then he ducked behind a city bus, and when it passed, he was gone.

20

Francisco collapsed on top of Reignbow's chest. It took him a moment to catch his breath, and when he did, he turned over onto his back. "I thought I was in good shape from basketball, but I guess not."

Reignbow laughed and pulled the blanket to cover her breasts. There was a chill in the room. The sweat on her chest cooled and made her skin goose up.

"Damn, I missed you so much," he said.

"Missed me? Past tense? We have sex, and now you're done missing me?" She poked him in the ribs. "You better be careful how you speak to a girl."

"Sorry. You know what I mean." Their breathing slowed and softened together. "You think we were quiet enough?"

"My mom doesn't care, Francisco. You don't think she knows?"

He shrugged. "I always try to be quiet here. You remember that dude Randy?"

"Yeah."

"You remember his girl, Shauna?"

"Yeah. Sort of, I guess."

"Did you ever hear why they broke up?"

She thought for a second. "No."

"Well, one night he snuck into Shauna's room and they started having sex, and her mom heard it. She marched in and dragged Randy's naked ass all the way across the apartment, threw him out the front door."

"Seriously?"

"Seriously. Didn't even hand his clothes back to him. And Randy lived, like, ten blocks away. Sprinted home naked. Had to scream up to his apartment for someone to let him in. The next day, he broke up with Shauna."

Reignbow laughed. "I would have paid good money to see that."

"Yeah, well . . . you never know, is what I'm sayin'. People go crazy. At my school, if they catch you having sex, they throw you out."

"Of the dorm?"

"Of the school."

"Just for having sex?"

Francisco nodded. Reignbow looked up to the ceiling and listened to the car horns on the street far below. The harsh traffic sounds seemed softer in the darkness. There was almost a melody to it. "It's nice to hear you open up about school. I was worried when you weren't talking about it, like you were hiding something bad."

"I'm not hiding anything." He studied her face, her ears, her cheeks. "Listen to this—if there's a girl in your room, they got a three-feet rule."

"Three feet?" She spread a yard between her hands.

"No. Three of these." He lifted his foot. "Between the two of you, there's got to be three feet touching the floor at all times. So that way, you can't lay down in bed together or nothing."

Reignbow squinted. "Just goes to show how for all their smarts at that school, they got no imagination."

"What d'you mean?"

"I can think of plenty of stuff to do with three feet on the floor."

"You can?"

Reignbow pecked him on the nose and started to sink down below the sheets.

"Yo, yo, Reign." He grabbed her by the shoulders and pulled her back up.

"What's wrong?"

"Nothing. It's just"—he checked his watch—"I got to go."

"What?"

"Yeah."

"Why?"

"Didn't you hear what I told Vincent? I got homework to do. Mountains of it."

"I thought that was just an excuse to get away from him!"

Francisco grabbed a pillow and whopped her in the face. "I wouldn't lie to Vincent! I don't lie to anyone."

"I know that." She shrugged and looked away.

"I'm sorry, Reign. But you don't know what it's like. It's not like public school."

He got out of bed and started getting dressed. She watched him—lifting his underwear, his pants, buttoning up his shirt. She got sad seeing less and less of his body.

"I wish you could stay here forever," she said. "Not go home. Not go back to school."

"I wish I could take you with me," he answered. "But I guess you'd never want to."

"You don't think I want to leave, too?" Her voice sounded harder than she'd intended. They stared at each other. It was the elephant in the room, and neither wanted to deal with it tonight. Or at all. He broke off her stare and slipped on his shoes. He gave her a peck on the cheek. "I'll see you tomorrow." Then he walked out, leaving her with nothing but her blanket, his scent, and the chill of the room.

21

His watch read 2:13 A.M. when he turned the deadbolt—
schtick—and tiptoed into his bedroom. Francisco's parents had
long since gone to sleep, and he sat down on his bed, rubbing
exhaustion from his face. Hard to believe, but it was a mere
nineteen hours ago that he woke up at school. Who knew
that tonight he'd be going to sleep in his old bed? The idea to
come home for Veterans Day weekend was an impulsive
one, struck at about eight o'clock yesterday morning when he
went to the student union for some breakfast and to check his
mailbox.

Each student had a mailbox used only for school mail. It
was a way for teachers to circulate notices and return papers
or tests to students. Francisco turned the numbers of his lock—
06-16-71, the digits of Tupac's birthday—and found a single
sheet curled up in his box. A math test he'd taken the day before. Francisco pulled out the test and saw a big red F written

at the top. Looking down at the ten questions, he saw that he'd gotten eight of them wrong.

It was a punch to the gut. Back at Alvarez, he'd never gotten less than a B on anything. And this wasn't even the first F he'd gotten so far at Seton Grove. Far from it. The student union kind of swirled around him, and it was almost in a fugue state that he found himself staggering to the nearby train station and boarding Metro-North for New York City. He desperately needed a break. Yes, he'd have to return in three short days when classes resumed, but three days at home would be like a tropical vacation compared to slogging through another hour up at boarding school.

Fighting to stay awake, curled up on his bed and digging out the math test, Francisco felt this was hardly a break. His eyelids were sticky from sleepiness. He began with the first question on the test, reading it, rereading it, and trying to figure out where he'd gone wrong.

Beep-beep-beep!

Francisco's head shot up, and he reached for the alarm.

Beep-beep-beep-beep!

He slammed the snooze button over and over, but the sound wouldn't stop. At the end of his bed, he noticed the phone flashing. The morning sun was starting to break through the window. Francisco rubbed his face, his right cheek dented from where he'd spent the night sleeping on his math text, and grabbed the phone.

"Hello?" he said.

"Fran?"

"Who this?"

"Who you think? Vincent."

"Oh. What's going on, bro? It's a little early—"

"No, it's late. Night's still going on." Vincent laughed.

Francisco checked his watch. "Six in the morning."

"Yeah, but I kinda never went to bed last night."

"Wild party, huh?"

"*Too* wild. Fran, listen, I'm in a little bit of trouble right now."

"Everything okay?"

"Not really. See, the thing is, I got my ass stuck in jail at the moment."

"*Jail?*"

"Can you believe that shit?"

"What happened?"

"Yo, nuthin' happened. But they got me locked up, and there's nothing I can say to convince them to let me out."

"Are you hurt?"

"No."

"Did someone else get hurt?"

"No! Did you listen to me? *Nothing* happened. But, yo, I need you, Fran. I'm gonna be in here for months while they get around to my case. I need you to bail me out. Please."

"Bail?" Francisco rubbed his eyes. "I can't believe I'm having this conversation right now. I feel like I'm dreaming."

"Ain't no dream. Come down here and see the shit. Jail's as real as it gets."

"Okay. Okay. How much is the bail?"

"Five hundred dollars."

"Oh, man. . . . I guess it could be worse."

"Whatever. Who knows? But for my broke ass, it might as well be a million."

"Do you even have that kind of money?"

"Are you kidding? Me?"

"Well *I* don't have it. Why would I have five hundred dollars?"

"I'm not saying you do. I'm just saying someone out there might."

Francisco went silent. The only thing worse than coughing up $500 was asking someone else to do it for you. He listened to the clanging of metal against metal in the background of the call. It sounded horrible.

"Yo, my phone time's about up. You gotta help me out, Fran. They gonna keep me here till next year."

"I don't know, V—"

"You don't *know?* Yo, if this was you, I'd be busting you out right now with a crowbar if I had to."

"All right. All right. I'm sorry. I'll think of something."

"Make sure you think fast. They got me locked up over at the Ninety-second Precinct."

Francisco grabbed a pen and scribbled "92nd Precinct" across his math test. "Got it. Don't worry. I'll see you soon, V."

"See you *sooner,* F."

22

November 10

"Well, look at what the cat dragged in," said Reignbow, grinning from the doorway. "You should have stayed last night like I asked. It would've saved you the trip this morning."

Francisco barely smiled. "Can I come in?"

"You okay?"

"Me? Amazing."

She gave him a quick peck on the lips. "You want something to eat?"

"Sure."

"My *casa*, your *casa*," she said, gesturing to the kitchen.

He hustled over to the refrigerator, opened the door, and tucked his body close inside the fridge like he was hiding between the covers of a book. There was a lie boiling in his guts, and it needed to come out fast. It seemed easier to do it while pretending to be distracted, when he didn't have to look her in the eyes.

"I don't see any food in here, Reign."

"There's Chinese leftovers."

He opened a couple white boxes and sniffed the contents. "Too spicy. You get everything spicy. How about delivery?"

"Okay."

"Okay, so I'll order in . . . if you could make me a little loan."

"For breakfast?"

"No, for, uh, five hundred dollars."

Reignbow came over and grabbed him by the shirt, pulling him away from the refrigerator. She slammed the door shut.

"Five hundred dollars for *what?*" she demanded.

"School."

"Are you serious?"

"For my books. Yeah."

"Books for five hundred dollars!"

"Well, and this scientific calculator I need for math class. Stuff like that."

"Did you just find out about this or something?"

"Yeah. Kind of. I got an e-mail from school this morning."

"But what about your scholarship? Doesn't that pay for your books?"

"No. The same way it doesn't pay for food. Scholarship is only for my tuition."

Reignbow scanned his face. She was looking for a sign— a smirk or something else to tell her that this was a joke. But his face was stony, serious. Scared, even.

"So why me, F? What makes you think that *I* have five hundred dollars?"

"Come on," he said, laying on a little charm. "Because you love me."

Reignbow laughed out loud. "Oh, really? Because I love you, I suddenly have five hundred dollars, huh?"

"Yeah. And also, with your mom on disability and every-thing. . . . Everyone knows how she is with money. She doesn't blow it." He felt dirty just thinking it. He felt filthy saying it. But he did it anyway.

"Right. Exactly. She doesn't blow it on dudes coming in here and asking for huge loans!"

"One year faithful to her daughter, and I'm just some dude?" he said, cracking a smile. Reignbow tried her very best to be hard on him, but a silly grin kept breaking through her lips. It was nearly impossible to be mad at him. He was the most sin-cere guy she'd ever known. "Plus, Reign, I promise to pay it back in a few months. Your mom won't even notice it's gone."

"So you expect me to lie to my mother?"

"No one's lying! It's just that no one's talking about it. There's a difference. C'mon. Five hundred dollars ain't a lot."

"So then why can't you get it?"

" 'Cause I don't work. And you know my moms likes to spend, so she don't have it either."

"And your little buddy of a friend Vincent can't help you out, because . . . why? That fool's always got some scheme cooked up, hustling money from one place or another."

The question threw Francisco. He had to think for a mo-ment. "Because we had an argument." He shrugged. "We had an argument, and we're not talking right now."

"Now *that* sounds like a lie."

"All right. You caught me red-handed."

"Uh-huh. So what's the money for?"

Francisco reached out one hand and slapped it with the other. "I'm a ba-a-a-ad boy."

Reignbow laughed. "Yes, you are. Now, what's it for? Honestly."

Francisco scratched his head. "No, really. That money is for school."

"Seriously?"

"Seriously."

She paused. "Okay. Let's *pretend* that I help you out and lend you the five hundred dollars. What do I get in return?"

"You mean like a box of candy?"

"No, way more than that. See, I'm lending it to you, so I'm expecting the money back, as promised. But I also want interest."

"What's the interest?"

Reignbow paused. It was like getting a wish from a genie. She'd better make it count. Grabbing his hand, she said, "Your time. Now, you can go and chill with your friends, you know I'm not trying to hold you back from that. But . . . not the whole weekend."

"All right."

"I know how much you wanted to go out with Vincent last night, but wasn't it nicer at my place?"

"Yeah. 'Course."

"Today's Saturday. You leave Monday. I do want to spend some of that time with you."

"That'd be nice."

She traced her finger across his chest. "So do you think you could maybe fit some time into your busy schedule to spend a few moments with me?"

"Of course," he said, pulling her close.

"Then do we have a deal?"

"Deal."

He kissed her forehead, her cheek, her lips. She didn't know it at the time, but they were Judas kisses.

"So breakfast. What do you want to eat?" she said.

Francisco felt elated. For one fleeting moment, the weight of the world was off his shoulders. "Everything," he said, grinning. "I feel like I haven't eaten for days."

Two hours later—after Reignbow snuck into her mom's closet, opened the Rainy Day box, and gave Francisco the money— Francisco and Vincent were walking out of the Ninety-second Police Precinct station.

"Yo, that was mission accomplished, bro," said Vincent. "Thank you." The two teens trudged up a hill going east across Third Avenue, headed back into Spanish Harlem. When they got far enough away, Vincent turned around and held up two middle fingers to Precinct Ninety-two. "Fuck the poh-lice!"

Francisco grabbed his arms and pulled them down.

"What in the hell are you doing?"

"Expressing my right to speak out!"

"You're full of it."

"Yeah, and they all can go fuck off."

"Let's just get out of here before they arrest you again."

Francisco hurried along the street, and Vincent walked behind with long, casual steps. "So what did they arrest you for, anyway?"

"Nuthin'! I didn't do nuthin'! I was just feeling upset, man. For real. Then . . . they arrested me."

"What were you upset about?"

"Just some stupid shit, man."

"What, last night? 'Cause we didn't hang out last night?"

"No. It was about a girl I met up with at the party. She really made me mad. But don't worry about it. It *is* funny, though, that a guy has to get himself locked up just to get your ass to come around."

"Oh, you're making jokes now?"

"C'mon, Francisco. What I did wasn't even that serious. For real."

"Then what'd you do?"

Vincent threw his arms up in the air. "I already told you! Man, those are some white cops in there. They lock you up for stupid shit."

"Stop lying, V. I'm your best friend. I bailed you out. You hafta tell me what you did."

"All right. Fine. I guess I kinda broke a car window. After I left the party."

"You *what*? Why? You steal a stereo?"

"No. I just saw the car parked there . . . I grabbed a rock and smashed the window. Broke it and ran off."

"Why the hell would you do that?"

Vincent had to think for a moment, then he got an

expression as if tasting something delicious. "I liked the sound it made. True story, F. I liked the sound. You shoulda heard it."

They passed through a tunnel and stopped on the Third Avenue side, waiting for car traffic to clear. Smelly water dripped around them from the old bricks holding up the overpass, forming mounds of green sludge on the ground. The Metro-North train rattled thirty feet overhead. It was the same train that Francisco would be taking upstate on Monday. The sound alone put a pit in his stomach.

"Vincent, I just don't understand you. You're getting all CIA on us again."

"So what? Then don't understand me. You don't understand nothin' nomore since you left New York."

"You seriously gonna be rude like that after I did you this favor?"

"I wouldn't have asked the favor if I'd knew you was gonna lecture me about it. What do I care? You shouldn't have bailed me out if it was so much trouble. I could have stayed in that motherfucker. It don't bother me."

"Oh, yeah? Then who was ever gonna bail you out?"

"Nobody, man! I would have been fine in there! Lock me up my whole life! Like I give a damn, sometimes."

"Vincent, you acting like a little kid right now. You need to grow the hell up."

Vincent jumped back, looking offended. "What you mean I need to grow up? You don't even know me nomore. You don't even live over here! You come to town, and I gotta hear about it from everyone else." Vincent waved him off, almost in tears. "Get out of my life, F. I'm good all by myself."

"V, I'm sorry I didn't call you. I am. But I did this other favor for you, and you ain't even gonna say thank you."

Vincent shrugged. "Ai'ight, fine. *Thank* you."

Francisco gave him a heavy look. "You mean it?"

"What the hell you want from me? Yeah, I mean it." Vincent took a breath, swallowed back his tears, chilled out a second. "Anyway, where'd you even get that money?"

Francisco paused, unsure if he should say it. "Reignbow. I got it from Reignbow."

"Hold up. Reignbow gave *you* money to bail *me* out?"

"Yeah."

"I can't believe she did that!" Vincent cleaned his teeth with his tongue. "Hang on. Tell the truth. She don't even know you bailed me out, does she?"

Francisco shook his head. "Not really. And you know how she'd feel about it, right?"

"Believe me, I know."

"So then you know she can't know, all right? You got to promise me you ain't gonna say nothing to her. Or anyone."

"Man, I ain't gonna say shit. We good."

"And one more thing," Francisco said, clapping his hands to emphasize the words. "You make your court date, all right? Don't miss that shit. Make sure you show up at court, and they'll give you the bond back. I gotta pay that back to Reignbow before her mom needs it, okay?"

"I got you."

"Good. Now lemme know how much you got me." Vincent reached out and shook Francisco's hand. "This ain't no joke," said Francisco.

"No, it ain't." Vincent looked penitent. Almost like a little boy. The cars on Third Avenue cleared out in front of them. They walked out of the tunnel and into Spanish Harlem. The streets were alive with people and noise.

"I'm sorry about all this, Fran. Things just went a little crazy for me last night, but I feel better now." Vincent smirked. "I'm officially out of the CIA."

"Good. Yo, but I gotta get some sleep now. You woke my ass up way too early."

"Hang out tonight, then?"

"Yeah."

"Call me. Promise. We get the Krew together and then we all go out."

"Francisco!"

Francisco groaned and twisted himself out of his sheets, checking his watch. Seven fifteen. The time alone meant nothing to him. Was it morning or night? He looked out the window and saw darkness.

Sitting up in bed, Francisco rubbed his face vigorously. Had he really slept away the whole day?

"Francisco? Are you okay in there?"

"Yes, Ma! Just a second please!" he hollered. He went to the mirror and looked at himself. There he was: Francisco Ortiz. Honors student. Basketball star. Liar.

Knock knock knock! "Francisco, please open the door!"

Francisco threw the lock and inched the door open. "What's going on, Ma?"

"Everyone's here to see you, honey. They've been here for an hour already!"

"Who is?"

"Didn't I tell you?"

"Tell me what?"

Viviana unfocused her eyes and put a delicate hand to her mouth. "Oh, my. Maybe I forgot. I invited Luisa over. And her husband and kids. Oh, and my aunt Maurina and her husband. And their kids, too. And some of the neighbors. . . ."

Francisco opened the door a little wider and checked down the hall, seeing a rather large crowd of people. "Mom. How many people are here?"

"Well, not many. Maybe twenty-five?"

"Twenty-five!"

Viviana gushed, "Oh, you're so loved, Francisco! I've been getting calls all day from everyone who wants to see you. I'm so sorry to wake you, I know how hard you work at that school. But like I said, they've been waiting for an hour or more . . ."

"All right. No problem."

Francisco pulled on a pair of pants and a shirt and headed into the living room, where he was greeted by a round of applause and cheering. He took a step back. Francisco wondered if this was what astronauts felt like. Everyone wanted to shake his hand. Francisco hadn't even gone that far: a four-hour train ride upstate. Boarding school was not outer space. But to people who had lived their whole lives in Harlem, maybe it seemed that way. Most of them had been to only two places: upper Manhattan and Puerto Rico. Francisco knew some folks who'd rarely been below One Hundredth Street, never seen Grand Central or the Empire State Building, except from a distance. They'd lived their whole lives in Spanish Harlem, and that was the place they'd die, too.

"Are you learning anything useful up there?"

"Have they ever met a Puerto Rican before?"

"Do you miss your parents?"

Francisco forced his smiles and answered as politely as he could. *Yes. No. Yes.*

They congratulated him, commended him, hugged him, told him stories of when he was a little boy reading to himself, clearly smart, and how they predicted he would one day be a success.

"Well, I'm not a success yet," he said humbly.

They posed for pictures next to him. It felt silly. Embarrassing. Francisco thought about how Vincent would have rolled his eyes over all of this attention—

Vincent!

Francisco had completely forgotten. He grabbed his mother's hand and whispered, "I'm supposed to meet Vincent tonight. When do you think I can leave?"

Viviana glanced around the crowd. "Well, your great-uncle Eduardo isn't here yet, and neither is the Ramirez family, and . . ." Francisco shook his head. "And I still have two dishes cooking in the oven." It was all the answer he needed. This was going to go on all night.

"All right, Ma. No problem." He found a quiet corner in the hallway and opened up his cell phone, pressing and holding down the number 2 till the phone rang.

"Yo, Vincent, it's me."

"I was worried for a second," said Vincent through the phone. "Didn't think you'd call."

"Listen, I'm sorry, but I can't come out with you tonight. My mom threw this party and didn't even tell me."

"Party? Can I come?"

"Believe me, Vin, you don't want to come. A bunch of old folks here. You'd hate it."

"So you're telling me that you're going to spend the night hanging out with old folks instead of chillin' wit' me?"

"No, I'm saying that maybe we can meet up later. They're old—how long can they party?"

"I don't know, F. And I also don't know how I feel about waitin' around for you to finish up your party so that you can come and *grace me* with your presence."

"What?"

"I mean, who do you think you are?"

"Nobody."

"Then why you acting like a king? Like it's impossible to hang out?"

Francisco took a breath. "I get it. I get why you feel that way. You're entitled. I just want you to see it from my perspective."

"It's getting harder and harder to see things from your perspective. It's like the only way to get you to hang out is if I'm in big trouble. Is that what it takes?"

"No. Of course not."

"Fran, you ever think about the old times?"

"Course I do."

"Yo, those were the best times in my *life*. I felt like we could do anything, go anywhere, and nothing mattered but having fun. We knew everyone, did everything. We wuz famous back then. But now? Life just sucks. I got nothin' to do except go to school, chill on the block. And I don't even go to school much anymore. Yo, life's gotten boring now, and I don't understand."

"It's 'cause we gettin' older. Making lives for ourselves. It can't always be like it was." Francisco looked up and saw his mother bringing over an old uncle of his, hobbling on a walker. "Listen, Vincent, this one's my bad. I gotta go." Francisco hung up.

Vincent pulled the phone away from his ear and punched a nearby mailbox. "Damn it!" Arguing with his best friend was the worst feeling in the world. It hurt him down to the soul.

He stood on the corner of 125th and Madison Avenue, in the middle of the action. Harlem central. Young men hawked watches and DVDs out of black garbage bags. Pimps, crazies, well-dressed folks with briefcases, mothers pushing strollers, and addicts all passed in the blink of an eye. It seemed like almost everyone was arguing into a phone. Everyone was broke, angry, desperate. Everyone was on the verge of being homeless; everyone was convinced they were six months away from multiplatinum success.

Vincent had never felt so alone among so many people. Harlem was supposed to be his home forever. You wanted to hear the best music in the world? Chill with the best kids? See the craziest things of your life? It was all happening in Harlem. He'd felt privileged, in a weird way, to be born in this ghetto.

But coming off that phone call from Francisco, feeling brushed aside, forsaken for a different kind of privileged life—the life of money, which was the only thing that Harlem never had much of—Vincent felt for the first time that his home was letting him down.

It simply sucked to be here.

He pulled out his phone and called Jason.

"Hello?" said Jason.

"Want to hang out?"

"Who is this?"

"Vincent, you idiot. What are you doing right now? Let's chill."

"I can't."

"Why not, yo?"

" 'Cause I'm with my dad. It's his court-appointed four hours with me. I gotta chill with him the whole four hours. I don't want to get anyone in trouble with the judge."

Vincent sighed. "Yo, I just talked to Francisco, and, Jason, you're never going to believe this, but that kid's turned white boy on us. He think we just some dumb colored kids. That's what he thinks of us now."

"That ain't true. Just chill, all right?"

"I can't chill. I'm so angry."

"Angry at what?"

"At what he thinks of me!"

Jason stopped talking. He was getting sick of Vincent's CIA routine.

"V?"

"What?"

"You gotta settle your shit down."

"What's that mean?"

"If Fran wants to think of me that way, then that's how I'm gonna be."

"How?"

"A stupid-assed ghetto kid."

"What? C'mon. You actin' seriously crazy now, V."

"Forget it."

"Vincent, don't do anything stupid."

"Yo, with the way I feel . . . fuck it." Vincent hung up.

He'd never felt more worthless in his life. Vincent thought about the posters hung up in the hallways of his school, spouting off with cheesy messages like

YOU CAN *DO* IT!
All your dreams are possible!

How much had they spent on those posters? For what? People want to know why there were so many problems in the ghetto? There was one reason, one cause: It was a *feeling*—it was this feeling that Vincent felt right now. *Worthless.*

Vincent's mind leapt to thoughts of mugging someone on the street, getting thrown back in jail. But he could imagine Francisco getting all high and mighty, trying to "teach him a lesson" by refusing to bail him out again, letting him sit in jail.

No, Vincent needed a better plan; he needed an angle. He racked his brain trying to think of something that took advantage of the secret that he shared with Francisco: their oath about the money.

For a moment, Vincent considered going straight to Reign-bow and telling her the truth. But what good would that do? Reignbow would hate on Francisco, which would be good for Vincent, but Francisco would also hate on Vincent, never talk to him again, and then disappear off to school.

School. Reignbow. These were the things that were taking Francisco away from him. These were the things that Vincent needed to eliminate from Francisco's life. A subtler plan was needed: a sweeping plan that would get him his best friend back—*for good*—so things could go back to the way they used to be. Back to the old times. Back when they were kids, brothers in a way, and nothing in the world could split them apart.

Vincent headed five blocks east to First Avenue. The sun had dropped out of the sky, and the Saturday street life, with all its busyness and noise, had taken firm hold of the 'hood. Vincent walked with long, swaggering strides, the kind of walk you needed to have if you were attempting to approach the notorious Witterberg Housing Projects unaccosted. Police cars parked permanently around the project's entrances. Sometimes there were cops positioned on the roofs, peering down with binoculars, rifles slung over their shoulders.

The Witterberg Projects was like an entire city, with food stores and day care centers and a health clinic. Inside, it teemed with thousands of families, screaming babies, hardworking couples, drug dealers, and the prostitutes who tricked out of some of the apartments. In the elevators, you'd find puddles of urine that never got cleaned up. Rumor had it that a dead body was found in a hallway once and it took two days before anyone came to pick it up.

Vincent jumped a fence and headed to the back of the main building, building 13, crossing a field of patchy grass littered with broken bottles. Kids flew past him on scooters through the dust. Ahead of him was a heavy black door, which was manned on either side by two large thugs. If you got past the thugs, then the door led to a concrete stairwell that went several stories down into the basement of building 13. Unlucky thirteen. Because that's where the boiler room was.

The boiler room wasn't a typical boiler room. Janitors knew enough to stay out. It had been co-opted as an office by a gangster named Boom. Boom was a short dude with little, gnarly teeth and big, droopy eyes. Boom wore a metallic, military-style vest, but it was too flashy and glittery to be real, and it would have made you laugh except for the dead-on intensity of Boom's face. No one ever laughed at Boom, at what he said or how he looked. He was the funniest-looking, least-funny guy you'd ever met.

The other reason you didn't want to laugh at Boom was the presence of his chief of security, RJ. RJ was a spastic, explosive kid in a dirty white tank top who talked so fast you thought he had a stutter, but it was just his tongue slapping his words at lightning speed.

Both of these guys were crazy, but in different ways. Boom was slow crazy; RJ was fast crazy. Boom was the type to kill your dog secretly in the middle of the night; RJ was the type to walk up to you in the middle of a crowd and just smash your face. Compared to these guys, even crazy-assed Vincent didn't seem so crazy anymore.

◆　◆　◆

DO NOT ENTER read the fire-engine red door.

One of the thugs knocked and pushed it open, poking his head into the boiler room.

"This dude sez he here to see you." Not waiting for an answer, the thug shoved Vincent into the boiler room and shut the door. Vincent stood there awkwardly, surveying the scene. Boom was sitting on a crate, staring at him. RJ was farther back in the shadows of the room, smoking a blunt.

"Who dis?" said RJ. "Who is you?"

"Vincent."

RJ cocked his head like a dog. "Do I know you, little nigga?"

Vincent shook his head. He was so scared that he could barely move. "I don't know."

"You don't know? Little nigga, I think I know you."

"Okay. Then you know me."

RJ got up and shoved Vincent in the chest. "Then why was you lyin' that you didn't know me?"

"What?"

Boom carved his hands between the two. "Relax. Relax. RJ, sit down. Vincent . . ." Boom grabbed another milk crate and set it next to him. "Have a seat."

The air was damp and putrid. Hulking machinery banged and echoed; broken pipes and chunks of insulation littered the ground. RJ took a seat on a steam pipe. The pipes in the projects weren't hot because the heat was almost never on.

Boom turned to Vincent. "So let's have ourselves a proper meeting. My brother, please, confess yourself: What you here for?"

"Yo, I need five hundred cash," said Vincent.

"That's a lot of money. What kind of trouble you in?"

"Who says I'm in trouble?"

Boom leaned forward and rotated his face back and forth for Vincent to see. "This ain't the kinda mug people come to when things are going good, you dig?"

"Yeah. All right, listen, I hafta handle some business. *Family* business. My brother needs money, and I'm helpin' him out. True story."

"You know I ain't the welfare office, right? You know my money ain't free?"

"I know that. But I ain't hard to find. Everyone knows me. True story."

Boom looked Vincent up and down. Vincent squirmed under the gaze of those weird, droopy eyes. Boom finally said, "All right. I'ma give you what you need, fool. But in return, you better have that money."

"No problem."

"Don't tell me no problem. Don't tell me nothing. Just have the money."

"Okay."

"And this loan comes with interest. Three and a half points per week, *every* week. So you better pay it fast. Got it?"

"That works for me."

"It does? Then you one stupid nigga. But that's that: Shit's too late, we have ourselves a deal." Boom pounded Vincent's fist.

A throaty chuckle emerged from the shadows. It was a

hideous sound, like a steam pipe springing a leak. "Stupid little nigga," said RJ. "Remember: You don't got no bread, then you don't got no breath."

"Listen to the man," said Boom, jabbing his thumb over his shoulder to RJ. "He's speaking truth to ears right now."

Boom closed his eyes and bobbed his head, listening to RJ's horrible threats as if they were some kind of great new rap. "We already have the body bag waiting for you, little nigga," said RJ, "with your name on it. It's ready to go. Pay us back, and you can keep it as a souvenir."

"I'll get you your money," said Vincent. "You don't have to threaten me."

Vincent was trying to act tough, but he was in the lion's den. And the weird thing was—what in the world was he doing there? Hadn't Vincent seen *Scarface* about a hundred times? Didn't he know what always happens when you take money from gangsters?

Of course. You didn't need to live in the ghetto to know that dealing with a guy like Boom was putting your life at risk. But that was exactly the point—that was what Vincent wanted: to put his life at risk. It was the only way, it seemed, to get Francisco to talk to him anymore. The more trouble Vincent got into, the more Francisco was forced to show up and save him. Francisco may have been trying to move on with his life, move away from the 'hood, start a new life, but if that plan meant leaving his old best friend, Vincent, behind, then Vincent wasn't going to allow it.

Boom wrote out a number on a piece of paper and handed

it to Vincent. "Give this to my man out by the monkey bars. He'll give you the money."

"Now dismiss yourself from our premises, fool," said RJ, pointing at the red door. "Dismiss yourself."

Vincent couldn't take it anymore. He whipped around to Boom. "I'm gonna pay the money back, but when I do," said Vincent, glancing at RJ, "I don't want *him* around."

RJ launched across the boiler room and got up into Vincent's face. "But I'm always here, fool! I'm gonna live in your dreams if I choose to. Now get out of my house! This here is the house of devils! And we *devils*! We devils!"

RJ picked up a brick and cocked it at Vincent. Vincent ran through the door and sprinted down a hall toward the stairwell. RJ threw the brick and it shattered against the wall by Vincent's head. RJ screamed out in laughter, and the laughter echoed up the metal stairs and followed Vincent all the way out the door of the building, until the big sky and cold, heavy wind destroyed the sound.

Vincent hoped he'd never hear it again.

The bills felt good balled in his fists, which he shoved into his pockets as far as he could. Five hundred dollars, cash money. Vincent felt sorry that he wouldn't be able to keep it in there for very long.

On the corner of 103rd and Park Avenue, he spied Reignbow emerging from a bodega. She was yammering with Boonsie and Dink, slurping Snapples and munching candy. Vincent forced a big ol' smile onto his dog-tired face and called out, "Reignbow! Yo, Reignbow! Hold up!"

Vincent ran across the street, dodging a gypsy cab. Reignbow caught sight of him and rolled her eyes. "Can *you* guys talk to him for me?" she whispered to her friends.

They nodded.

Vincent bounded up and gave the girls hugs. He was acting insanely chipper. "Hey, what's good, yo? How's the three prettiest girls in Spanish Harlem doin'?"

Dinky and Boonsie laughed.

The girls never admitted it, but Vincent was actually pretty cute. His body was tall and athletic; his eyes were quick and sparkling, and he always appeared to be on the verge of telling a joke. Except for Reignbow and Francisco, no one in the Krew dated each other. But it was a secret that Dinky and Boonsie both had minor crushes on Vincent.

"Haven't seen you all day," said Dink. "What you up to, Vin?"

"You know me. Nuthin', nuthin' at all. . . . Except listen, I'm glad I ran into you girls. Especially you, Reign."

"Oh yeah? And why's that?" she said, crossing her arms and squinting her eyes.

"Because I been meaning to give you this."

He pulled out the messy handful of bills and pushed them into her hands.

"There you go," he said.

"Damn!" yelled Boonsie, shocked to see so much money.

"What's this?" said Reignbow.

"I'm returning the favor."

"What favor?"

Vincent acted offended. "That's five hundred dollars right there!"

Dinky butted in. "What favor? What favor did you do?"

"For bailing me out of jail," said Vincent. "That's what."

Reignbow's mouth fell open.

Dinky howled, "You got locked up!"

"Yeah, I got locked up. So what?"

"Yo, I never know nothin' around here," squealed Dinky. "Why'd you get locked up?"

Vincent laughed. "It was over some bullshit."

Dinky persisted. "Then why won't you tell us?"

" 'Cause it wasn't even that serious. Look, I'm just givin' it back to Reign——"

"Where'd you get this money from?" Reignbow demanded, with fire in her throat.

"Huh?"

"You heard me!" She grabbed his shirt and yanked him, but he easily moved her hand away.

"Please. Don't worry about where I got it from. You know what I'm saying? I'm just returning the loan back. 'Cause if it wasn't for you, Reignbow, I would've been in there eating some dried cheese and bread, man."

Reignbow's head spun.

Dinky took a slurp off her drink. "I wouldn't have never bailed you out."

Vincent laughed and poked at Dinky. "Yo, stop hanging out with this girl, Reign."

"You never tell me none of your stories! So why should I bail you out?" Dinky said.

"What stories? Oh, man. Listen, Reign, tell Francisco to highlight me and all that. Ai'ight? I'm gonna head up outta here. *Thank you* again, ai'ight?"

He stared at Reignbow a moment too long. He was messing with her, yeah, but he was honestly thankful, too. In a way, she had given him much more than five hundred dollars: She'd given him an edge in Francisco's loyalties. Francisco was, more than ever, a competition between them; something to be stolen away from the other—to be won.

Vincent strutted off down the street yelling back to the girls, "See me on the block, yo!"

Dinks let out a long whistle and turned to Reignbow, who looked like she'd seen a ghost. "Yo, Reign. What's wrong?"

"He lied to me," she growled.

"Who?"

"Francisco. I gave *Francisco* the money. And he dead-assed lied to me."

"What did he lie to you about?"

"About the money! He said that it was for something else."

"Well, clearly it was for Vincent," Boondangle said.

Reignbow glared at the stupid girl. "Shut the hell up, Boon."

Dinky stepped in between them. "Okay, that's enough. Let's just go. We have better things to do than argue."

"Hang on," Boondangle persisted. "Vincent needed the money. He's one of the Krew. Why shouldn't Francisco help him out?"

"Because F's gotta lie about it? I mean, what's good with that?"

"He wouldn't have had to lie if he didn't think you'd be so uptight."

"I'm not uptight!"

"No, you're just a bitch."

"Oh, damn!" yelled Dinky.

"Go to hell," said Reignbow, throwing up her arms. "I'm gone."

She stormed away, cursing. Random folks walking by stared at her; a few laughed at how mad she looked. Dinky shook her head at Boonsie.

"I can't believe you, Boons."

"Me?"

"Yes, you! Every time you open your mouth, it's problems!"

Boonsie crossed her arms and looked away. Dink sighed and was helpless to do anything more than watch her friend disappear down the street.

28

The sounds of Francisco eating had never annoyed her before. But it did now. *Scraaaaaaape!* He scraped the bottom of a large pot, emptying out the last grains of rice onto his plate. *Scrape scrape scrape!* It was leftovers from the family get-together earlier tonight, which had ended hours ago, leaving behind ransacked armies of plastic cups half-filled with beer, and lipstick-marred napkins creeping wounded across the apartment.

Francisco smiled across the table at Reignbow. "You want some food? There's tons more in the fridge."

"No."

"How's your day been going?"

She said nothing. On the table between them was a centerpiece: a large, ornately painted ceramic bowl full of water. Submerged in the water were strands of leafy kelp, and mixed in with the kelp were three or four floating dollar bills. Old-country Puerto Ricans believed that these centerpieces were enchanted, that money would grow from the leaves and make the family rich. Reignbow looked at the bowl and shook her head. Her mom used to have one of those, too.

What a joke, thought Reignbow. Everyone in the 'hood is scraping for money, but here were some folks waiting for it to grow on trees. Or in the weeds. It was so stupid that it made Reignbow hate being Puerto Rican, hate being from the ghetto, and hate being poor.

"Reign? You all right?"

She shrugged.

"So how was your day?"

"It was okay, I guess. I don't know. . . ."

"Okay, you guess, or you don't know? Which is it?" He smiled, meaning it as a joke. But it was just enough smart-ass to make Reignbow flip out. She pulled out Vincent's wad of money and threw it on the table.

"What's that?" he asked.

"You don't know?"

"What is this?"

"Count it."

Reluctantly, he did. He sighed and put it back down. You'd never seen someone so unexcited about handling five hundred dollars. "Who gave you this?"

"Well, you see, it's actually a funny story. I was just over on 103rd, and *Vincent*, of all people, came up to me and just out of nowhere starts thanking me for lending him five hundred dollars."

Francisco lifted his cup of juice and drank, hiding his face behind it.

"But you see, F, I don't remember lending *Vincent* five

hundred dollars. I remember lending *you* five hundred dollars. For books. I'm waiting, Francisco. I'm waiting for you to explain yourself. I'm giving you more than a fair chance."

"Reign," Francisco said slowly, "I have no idea—"

"Yes you do! And if you honestly don't know, then show me the money I loaned you. Show it to me right now! You must still have it. It's not like you already bought your books."

Francisco went stone quiet.

Reignbow smiled bitterly. Her point was proven. "Your life is going in a different direction than Vincent's. You got a lot to lose now, and Vincent is just a . . . loser. He's dragging us both down."

"If I had told you the truth, you would have never given it to me, Reignbow."

"Francisco. Come on."

"I was just helping somebody out. Helping out my best friend."

"If he's your best friend, he wouldn't have asked you to get into trouble for him. If he was your best friend, he would have forgiven you for telling him no."

Francisco shook his head.

"Let me explain something," said Reignbow. "You're a kid from Harlem with a good shot in life. But I hope you're not taking it for granted. I hope you're not taking *me* for granted."

Francisco looked off in pain.

"What's gonna happen to us, F?"

"What d'you mean?"

"You promised nothing would change."

"It won't."

"But it already has. You never would have lied to me before. I mean, what else has changed with you? Remember all those talks we had about our future together? What happens if you decide that you don't want to come back to New York after school?"

Francisco shrugged. "I don't know. You tell me. You're the one who has my whole life figured out." He glared at her. "What are *you* going to do after you graduate, Reignbow? Hmm? Do you want to stay in Spanish Harlem? Are you gonna stay, or you gonna leave?"

"You know my situation, F. With my moms being sick—"

"But what do *you* want to do? Are you ever going to leave here?"

Reignbow glared at him. A voice inside her head screamed, *How can you doubt that! Of course I want to leave!* But getting out was more complicated for her than it was for him. She searched his face for understanding, which she did not find. So she chose to say nothing.

"Then it sounds like you're going to stay," Francisco continued. "And if you stay, and if we're going to stay together, then that means I have to come back after graduation. But, Reign, isn't that just holding me back, too? Aren't *you* just holding me back?" Francisco slammed down his spoon. "I'm feeling pressure from all over like you wouldn't believe, Reign! And this isn't helping!"

He grabbed the wad of money and threw it across the table. He meant to throw it right at Reignbow, but the wad fell short and landed in the money bowl. It splashed Reignbow's shirt.

"Goddammit, Francisco!" She grabbed a towel and patted at her shirt. "You're such an asshole."

"Yo, that's it. I got to go before I hit something." He stomped toward the front door. Reignbow watched him go, a question on her lips. Francisco stopped and pivoted. "Wait, this is *my* apartment! You leave."

Reignbow stared, gauging him. "Are you serious? Are you really throwing me out?"

"Yeah."

Reignbow looked deep into his eyes. "You're angry, F. You're just angry. Nothing more." She stood up. "I'll go. That's fine. And I'll forgive you this one time, because I know that it's nothing but anger coming from you right now."

Reignbow walked toward the door. Francisco followed her with his eyes. She paused as a thought occurred to her.

"I guess it was bound to happen," she said.

"What?"

"Our first fight."

Francisco nodded.

"It sucks," she said. "I had no idea it would suck so much." Then she walked out.

Francisco listened to Reignbow's steps going down the hall. Then he listened to the elevator doors open and close. He listened to the silence. The entire time, he kept believing that she was going to turn around and come right back to him. When she didn't, Francisco kicked over one of the dining room chairs. Then he grabbed his coat and headed out the door.

Francisco looked up and down the streets for Reignbow, but she was nowhere. He sighed and pulled out his cell phone. He typed in *V–I–N*, and a picture of Vincent came up. Francisco gripped the phone hard and shook it, giving the little Vincent a strangle. Then he released his grip, felt somewhat more calm, and hit the green *Call* button.

Later that Saturday night, close to midnight, Francisco's mom, Viviana, came home. She'd spent all evening visiting with a sick aunt who couldn't make it to Francisco's party. Viviana brought over proud pictures of her son to show. But the old aunt didn't care to look at the pictures, and instead spent hours talking Viviana's ear off about the problems of the world today, and ordering Viviana around to complete chores that the aunt herself couldn't do. Changing lightbulbs. Running loads of laundry. Viviana didn't mind helping out, but the whole evening sure was a test of one's patience.

When she finally got home and finished cleaning up her own apartment, Viviana pulled a plate of roasted vegetables out of the fridge and sat down at the table. She plopped down in the chair with her cold leftovers and her weary thoughts. "Lordy, lordy," she said to herself, rubbing her temples.

Viviana stabbed a piece of broccoli and gnawed on it. It had turned rubbery in the fridge. She managed to swallow down the ugly piece and slammed her fork on her plate. Disgusting. It was right at that moment when Viviana happened to look into the money bowl. At first she didn't know what she was looking at, then she screamed. Viviana jumped up so fast she knocked the table askew. Plunging her hands into the water, she reached between the leaves of kelp. One by one, she pulled twenties and fifties out of the water.

"It's a miracle! A miracle!" she cried hysterically. "We've been blessed!"

Within minutes, five hundred dollars in soaking-wet bills lay in front of her. Viviana grabbed a hair dryer from the bathroom and blasted them with gusts of hot air. She profusely thanked God, Mother Mary, and Jesus, over and over, wiping tears from her eyes, and pocketed the bills one by one as they dried.

Dollar signs encrusted in diamonds.

The letters *MVP* in platinum.

Necklaces. Rings. Earrings. Bling.

"Damn, man. I can see myself wearing all this stuff."

Vincent was standing in front of a jewelry store window, his face pressed against the glass looking at the displays. Francisco stood away a step, a little less impressed and a lot more distracted.

"Fran, let's go in."

"You don't have any money."

"So?"

"So you got no business being in there."

"Yo, I got business being anywhere I want."

Vincent pulled on the door of the jewelry shop, but it was locked. He saw people inside the shop, so he yanked a few more times.

"Buzz me in! You still open!" Vincent yelled through the

glass. The owner looked Vincent up and down. Vincent looked half crazy and half homeless. He was wearing a T-shirt even though there was a cold wind tonight and a little bit of rain coming down.

The owner shook his head no.

"Motherfucker!" yelled Vincent. "You just lost my business!" He slammed the glass hard. The owner ignored Vincent and turned to a young Hispanic couple already standing at the counter. The Hispanic boyfriend was pointing at a jeweled necklace in the display case, while the guy's girlfriend looked at Vincent through the window and gave him a smile that was partway flirtatious and partway like *you don't have a chance*.

"Shit," said Vincent. "Sometimes it's like the whole world's against me."

Francisco looked up at the night sky and held out his hand. "Yo. The rain's coming harder."

"So what?"

"So let's get some cover. I wanna talk to you."

The boys ran across the street to a covered doorway. They tucked inside and watched the city shuffle past them. Vincent entertained himself by harassing people on the street, asking some of them for the time, some of them for money. He spoke gibberish to others just to get a look of confusion from them. This made him laugh. Then Vincent saw a pretty Hispanic girl, who looked like she was dressed for an office job, walking by herself.

"Yo, Mama, how about I take out you for the night of your life?"

She gave him a double glance before moving on quickly.

"Damn!" Vincent laughed. "You see that body on her?"

The rain fell harder. People stopped passing by and the streets turned quiet except for the taxis, full of wet-looking passengers, splashing the city's runoff all over the sidewalks.

Francisco turned to his best friend. "Yo, Vincent, why'd you fuck me over?"

"Why'd I what?"

"Fuck me over."

"Fuck you over how? What'd I do?"

"You got me in trouble."

"Huh?"

"With Reignbow. You got me in trouble with her."

"How I got you in trouble?"

"You gave her back the five hundred, you idiot!" Francisco smacked Vincent on the head.

"Oh, thaa-a-at. Right. Listen, Fran, I had to pay her back."

"No, you didn't! You promised me you wouldn't tell her!"

"Yeah, but it was a lot of money, and I didn't want her getting worried about it. It was a big favor she did."

"Yeah, a favor to *me*, not you."

Vincent cartoonishly smacked his own forehead. "Yo. I'm sorry, ai'ight? I must've forgot."

"What? How could you forget!"

"I just have a lot on my mind lately. . . ."

Francisco shook his head, unconvinced.

"So is she mad at you?"

"Yeah!"

"Does she forgive you?"

"Eventually, I guess she will."

"So then what's the problem, F?"

"The problem is you hurt her bad. And you made *me* hurt her." Francisco shook his head.

"I'm sorry. True story. But you gotta believe me I was only trying to do the right thing."

"Well, stop. You ain't any good at doing the right thing. You're only good at doing the wrong thing."

Vincent laughed. "You got a point there, Fran. More than you know. See, true story: I'm in serious trouble now."

"What d'you mean?"

"Do you have any idea where I got that money?"

"No."

Vincent pointed uptown. "Witterberg Projects. That nigga Boom."

"Boom?"

"Or whatever he calls hisself." Vincent spat into the street.

"That dude's a serious gangster."

"I guess so. Far as I saw it, he was just a guy with money, ya dig? But now I gotta pay this dude back."

Francisco ran his hands through his hair. He was trying not to panic. "I can't believe it. That's so messed up, Vincent."

"I know, I know. But I *had* to pay Reign the money back. I mean, you're like my brother, right?"

"Of course. But owing this guy Boom ain't like owing me. I mean, *I'm* not gonna break your legs over it."

"I know. I know."

"Did you get a court date yet? Because as soon as you get the bond back, you can pay him with the bond money—"

"No, no, no. Boom's gonna need the money way before then. And anyway, I'll owe him interest, too."

"You gotta use your brain sometimes, Vincent!" Francisco dug his finger at the side of Vincent's head. "Where's your mind at? When you gonna learn that I'm not always gonna be there for you?"

Vincent nodded. "I dig. I dig. I mean, that's cool. Then I guess I'll just let the nigga find me . . . and go off with my head 'cause I couldn't pay that shit on time."

Francisco felt like his head was going to explode. It was just *one more thing*. He'd come home from school like a soldier from war, seeking rest, recovery, seeking the comfort of the trappings of home—friends, family, home cooking.

But all he'd found here, around every corner, were people who needed him. Who were relying on *him*. His mom was relying on him to lift the spirits and satisfy the curiosities of extended family and old friends. His dad was relying on him to be a good—no, great—ambassador of everything Puerto Rican. Reignbow was relying on him to go out and become a success *while* staying close to home, which seemed contradictory. Vincent was relying on Francisco to be his same old self, the guy who would give up everything for his best friend. Well, that was fine back when they were hooligans and had nothing. But now Francisco had something to lose: his future.

Francisco looked into his best friend's eyes. Bright, alive, and fiery with desperation. For a split second, Francisco imagined Boom killing Vincent. He imagined returning to New York for the funeral and what those dark eyes would look like with no life in them, staring up at Francisco. The thought shook him to his core.

"Naw, ain't no one gonna go off with your head."

"Why?" Vincent's eyes lit up. "You got a plan?"

"Better than that: I got the money. The original five hundred. It's at my place."

Vincent took Francisco by the shoulders and hugged him. "I don't know how, and I don't even want to ask. But I'm moved, bro. I really am."

"Good. You owe me big-time for this."

"I owe you *everything*, ai'ight? So do you think you can get that shit now?"

"Yeah, *right* now. The sooner this is done, the sooner I can start to enjoy my vacation. I didn't come down from school to deal with all this stress. They got plenty of stress up there for me."

Francisco sprinted home, catching himself yawning as he ran. Inside his apartment, he flicked on the fluorescent kitchen light and went straight for the centerpiece bowl. As the brownish yellow overhead warmed up and snapped to a buzzing brightness, Francisco pulled up handfuls of the large leaves. Water ran between his fingers back down into the bowl. But there was no money in the water. The money was gone. He searched through the leaves a few times to make sure, then collapsed in a chair and, with his head in his hands, tried to figure out what happened. The only explanation he could come up with was that Reignbow took it back. While he was busy ingeniously throwing himself out of his own apartment, she must have taken the cash. He didn't blame her—it was hers, after all.

Either that or the leaves in the bowl somehow ate the money.

Regardless, everything in Francisco's life just became a lot more complicated. It took a few seconds for him to muster the will to make the phone call, but as soon as Vincent picked up, Francisco came straight out and said it. "Yo, Vin, we got a major problem."

30

November 11

For much of the next morning—Sunday morning—Reignbow's phone rang and rang. Reignbow promised herself she wasn't going to pick up, but she also wasn't going to turn it off. She liked seeing Francisco's name lighting up her phone every five minutes. She liked the fact that he was suffering. It gave her some pleasure.

When her mother finally screamed, "Reignbow! Would you either answer that thing or shut it off?" all Reignbow did was turn the ringer volume down. It wasn't until about his fortieth call that she decided he'd been punished enough and picked up.

"What."

"Reign!" he almost yelled. "You answered!"

"Yes. Now what do you want?"

"Want . . . ? It's me, Francisco."

"I know," she said flatly. "Can't you hear the excitement in my voice?"

"Yo, Reign, don't be like that. Where you at?"

"I don't know. Depends on what you want."

"I want to see you."

"Why?"

"Why? Because you're my girl, Reign."

"You want to apologize to me, then?"

"Apologize?"

"Yeah."

"Yo, hang on right there. Maybe *you* should be the one apologizing to me. You were the one who came up in my face."

"Yeah, and *you're* the one who threw me out."

Silence. Then more silence.

"Reignbow?"

"Uh-huh?"

"I love you. You know that, don't you?"

"Yeah. So?"

"So, I was just feeling mad at the time. Like you said. But I'm not mad anymore. I'm calling because I want to see you. Ai'ight?"

"That's not quite an apology, Francisco, but I guess it's close. And believe me, I'm not smiling. But ai'ight. I'll take it. Listen, I'm going to be at the Thing with my girls in an hour. See you there?"

"Yeah. See me there."

Francisco hung up the phone.

The Thing? he thought. Francisco hated the Thing. The rumor around Spanish Harlem was that the Thing was supposed to be art. Sculpture, or something. A so-called installation artist built it in the middle of Jefferson Park, over on 112th Street. It was fifteen feet tall and made of giant metal sheets cut into circles and triangles. Imagine a jungle gym that's impossible to use, that would cut you to shreds if you tried.

The only good thing about the Thing was that it was an easy place to meet up. An hour after her phone call with Francisco, Reignbow, Dinky, and Boondangle were hanging out at the Thing. A guy they knew named Tony was hanging around, too, bugging them. That's how it worked at the Thing. Hang out there, and you ran into everybody.

Tony's idol was 50 Cent, and Tony was always talking about him—50 this and 50 that. Wake up Tony in the middle of the night, and he'd sit right up and say, "Yo, what about 50?" Stop him in the street, and he'd just start talking 50, out of the blue.

"Well, what do you think about 50?" Tony asked the girls. "D'you consider him a sexy rapper?"

Reignbow shook her head. "Tony, seriously, what's up with you and 50?"

"For real!" said Dinky. "Do *you* consider him a sexy rapper?"

The girls laughed.

Tony protested, "No! But you know, he got shot and all that."

"So what?" said Reignbow. "That's news?"

"Tony just likes him because he think he looks like him," chimed in Boonsie. Everyone laughed, because Tony did kind of look like him.

"Plus, getting shot nine times ain't sexy," said Dinky.

"I know it ain't, but he still alive and all that."

Dinky talked over him. *"Getting shot nine times ain't sexy!"*

Tony tried to defend himself. "But—"

"Let's talk about how I'm a better rapper than you, Ton," said Dinky, who started dancing some cool, jerky moves around the Thing. The girls laughed their heads off. The morning wind was cold. The trees were bare.

Then Dinky looked across the street and hollered out, "Yo yo! *Vincent! Francisco!*"

The two boys were coming across the street. Francisco smacked Vincent across the chest.

"Yo, Vin, I want you to play everything cool, ai'ight? I need to make up with her first. I ain't gonna trick her no more."

"I got you. No problem."

"No one needs to hear you spouting off. Don't go telling war stories from jail."

"What war stories? I got no good stories. They make sure to keep that shit nice and bland inside."

"Good. And that's how I want you, too. Nice. Bland."

Vincent gave him an off-center look, then busted out laughing.

"What?" said Francisco.

"Man, that's the whitest thing you ever said. I got all encouraged and shit when I heard some ai'ight's slipping out of your mouth again. It took a couple days . . . but *this?*"

Vincent laughed again and Francisco playfully shoved him.

"Yeah, and you're like King Ghetto, right?"

Vincent's face turned serious. "What'd you call me?"

"King Ghetto. So what?"

"Why'd you call me that?"

"I don't know. I was joking."

"Joking, huh? What if I called you King Snob?"

"Yo, V, chill out."

"No. That shit hurt my feelings, Fran."

Francisco waved him off and kept on walking. "Yo, you're impossible these days."

By the time they arrived at the Thing, there was definitely a mood going on. There was tension between Reignbow and Francisco, and tension between Francisco and Vincent. Everyone could feel it. While Vincent was kind of sulking to the side looking at Francisco, Francisco and Reignbow were kind of looking at each other sideways—a little shy and still a little angry.

Dinky looked at Tony. "Go over there and play ball or something. This conversation is gonna be between our Krew."

"But why I gotta leave?"

" 'Cause it's private, I said!"

"It's like that, huh? What would 50 do?" asked Tony.

"Why don't you go find him and ask!"

Vincent shifted his gaze from Francisco to Reignbow, back and forth. He made up his mind about something dark and skulked over to Reignbow. Pulling on her sleeve, he said in a hushed tone, "Yo. Yo, Reignbow . . ."

"Uh-huh?"

"I'm gonna need that five hundred dollars back."

"What?"

"I'm gonna need that money back. True story."

"What for?"

"I gotta pay this dude off. This stupid-scary dude."

"Are you serious?"

"Yeah!"

"Get out of here, Vin."

"Get out? I'm gonna be dead, Reign."

"You being dead is your problem, not mine."

Vincent growled. "You cold, Reign. Antarctic." Then he pointed over to Francisco. "Yo, get over here, Fran. Tell your girl to do this thing for me."

"I can't believe you're having this conversation right now," muttered Francisco, who looked more sad and depressed than mad. He shook his head like a big ol' buffalo and precariously climbed to the top of the Thing. He sat high up in the wind, the solitude, gazing across the city while his friends argued.

"Vincent, you need help," said Reignbow. "You need serious help."

"Fran, tell her I need that five hundred. She's tryin' to play me right now, you see this? Come over here."

"Yo," said Reignbow, "tell him to get out of my face."

Then Boonsie butted in. Even she was getting frustrated. "Vincent, maybe you should get a job instead of mooching off your friends."

"Guys! Guys!" yelled Dinky, shutting up everyone. "Stop it! Francisco's leaving town tomorrow night, and we're spending this time arguing. Now, Vincent, can you please shut up and go somewhere till this cools off? We fightin' so much lately, and I hate it."

Reignbow nodded. "Dink's right. Let's get out of here, F. I gotta get away from this kid."

"No," said Francisco. "Things won't cool off until this shit is figured out."

"And how we gonna figure it out?" she said.

"I don't know. . . . Give him the money."

"What?"

"You have the money, Reign," said Francisco. "Give it to him, and we're done."

"How dare you side with him!"

"I'm not siding with anyone. I just need some peace and quiet."

"Well, I don't have the five hundred!" yelled Reignbow.

"I know you have it. You took it out of the money bowl."

"I didn't take shit!" She wiped away a few tears.

Vincent danced around like a maniac. "See, Reign, you ain't got his number no more. He done with you."

"Shut up, bro," yelled Francisco, pointing. "I'm sick of you."

"*Me?*" said Vincent.

"Yeah. You crazy, and it's making *me* crazy. I can't deal with either of you anymore."

"Oh, I'm crazy, huh?" Vincent said.

"Yeah, you are. Didn't I say don't talk about the money?"

"You said don't talk about *jail*." Vincent raised his arms like he was free and clear. "I didn't mention nothin' about *jail*."

"Well, I don't need this shit nomore! I'm sick of this place. This damned 'hood . . . I hate it. I hate it here!"

"Yo, yo, yo," said Vincent. "Be careful what you sayin'. This is where you from. We're your people."

"It's where I *was* from. And if you're my people, then I don't want any goddamn people. I'm outta here."

He jumped off the Thing. Reignbow grabbed Francisco's arm and spun him around. They were about ten feet away from everyone else, on the other side of the sculpture.

"I can't believe you said those things, F."

"Neither can I," he muttered.

"So can we talk about this later? This evening. Please?"

"I'll think about it."

"Can you come by my place?"

"We'll see, I said." He shoved her hand and stormed away.

Vincent cupped his hands to his mouth and yelled, "You abandoner! Abandoner! Let me die, huh!"

Francisco kept on going. Vincent got into Reignbow's face and yelled at her, "See what you did!"

The girls ganged up on Vincent, whacking him and yelling, "Look what *you* did!"

Dinky shoved Vincent's head. "You not thinkin', man."

He touched his hair gingerly, feeling all around it. "Ow! She touched the waves . . . she touched the waves!"

"Yeah, I did touch the waves. You got money for your hair, but you don't got money to pay a debt back?" Dinky shouted.

Reignbow looked dazed, feeling like the earth might slip out from under her, send her spinning off into space, past airplanes, toward Mars. But her anger brought her back down hard, and she grabbed Vincent's shirt collar in her fist. "Are you happy now?"

Vincent gave her a terrible look. He looked mad and worried and scared, all at the same time. She let go. Girls like to get tough with guys sometimes because they figure a guy can't really do anything about it, like hit them. But Vincent was different. He actually *would* hit a girl. So Reignbow backed off, turning around and walking away. It was her third argument with one of the Krew since Francisco got home—she didn't want any more.

And the thing is, she'd get her wish. It would be her last argument ever with Vincent. In fact, it would be the last time she'd ever see him.

Francisco looked at himself in the mirror. He didn't recognize the monster looking back. He wanted to hide—not so much from himself but from everyone else. Namely, his friends. They'd never forgive him for what he said. Why should they?

Francisco grabbed the faucet knob and had to strangle it to get it to budge. It squeaked before releasing a thin stream of cold water. He cupped the water and drank some, then washed his face.

It was Sunday evening in the city. The hour was magical. There was still some light in the sky, and the streetlamps were just flickering on. An amber glow washed gently across the blacktop. The city could be so ugly one moment and turn incredibly beautiful the next.

He guessed Reignbow was waiting for him. At this exact moment, she was probably home expecting him to knock on her door, sweep her into his arms, apologize for everything, and kiss her. He guessed, also, that he wouldn't have the courage to do anything except disappoint her.

But—in fact—she wasn't thinking any of that. She wasn't thinking about Francisco at all. She was home with her mother, watching *The Voice* on TV. A Chinese takeout carton sat on her lap, untouched. She was thinking about the money. No matter what Francisco said, she knew it still had to be in his apartment. Her mom's rainy-day money, *years* of savings, stuck in someone else's place.

And it was all her fault.

Reignbow closed the lid on her moo shu pork and bent forward, feeling like she was going to throw up.

"You all right, honey?" said Lily, seeing Reignbow's pale complexion.

"Yeah. I just don't feel well right now."

"Me neither. Look at these folks singing. They're good, but you're way better. I can see you on that stage right now."

Reignbow couldn't see herself anywhere but in a whole mess of trouble. Viviana probably had the money, and Reignbow knew there was no way in the world she could get it back. Asking for it would bring to light Reignbow's having taken the money in the first place. All she could do was pray that the rainy-day fund wouldn't be needed—at least not until Reignbow was older and moved out of the house and far from shouting range when her mom eventually discovered it.

Meanwhile, Francisco was getting dressed in his bedroom, taking off his baggy jeans and putting on khakis. He slipped a button-down shirt across his back and looked in the mirror as he tucked it in. Finally he took out his cell phone and placed it on his desk. He looked at it for a moment, tapped his chin with his forefinger, then walked away. For anyone who ever knew him—Reign, Vincent, kids he used to go to school with at Alvarez—he would be unreachable. They could call his cell, but it would only buzz around on his desk uselessly.

The lights were off, and the living room was dark. Francisco found his parents on the couch watching TV. The remote drooped in Viviana's hand; her eyes were glazed while she watched the screen. His dad was asleep. The whole apartment felt unbearably lonely.

"Ma," said Francisco. He stood over her with his bag slung over his shoulder. But she didn't hear him. Some home video contest show was on TV, and silly white boys were flipping each other out of catapults and landing on houses. The studio audience was laughing and applauding.

"Ma!"

Viviana startled. She looked up with a tired expression, her eyes red and strained from watching TV in the darkness.

"Yes, honey?"

"Ma. I'm leaving."

Viviana didn't react at first. The words took time to settle in.

"Where are you going? To Reignbow's?"

"No. To the train. I'm going back to school tonight."

"You're leaving tonight? *Now?*" Her eyes got big, and tears came into them. Francisco had to look away from her hurt. "But I thought you were going tomorrow—"

"No, I got classes tomorrow morning," he said. He was

picking at his hand, a piece of dry skin on his knuckle, avoiding her eyes. "You got my days mixed up."

"Oh! Oh, my goodness. Honey, already?" She stood up and snaked her arms around her son. "You're leaving now? This *minute*?"

"Mm-hm."

"Oh, my."

"I have to catch the last train."

"When am I going to see you again?"

"Maybe Thanksgiving. Or I might stay at school then. So I guess Christmas?"

"Ernesto! Wake up! My baby's leaving! We won't see him for months!"

Ernesto stood and watched his wife hugging their son in the darkness. His son's body hulked over Viviana's small, round frame. Ernesto nodded to himself, preparing for all the tears yet to come from his wife over the next several days, all the things she'd say about missing their son, and all the reassurances he'd have to give her. Ernesto would miss the boy, too, terribly, but his job was to listen to Viviana. Listen to her as she got it all off her chest.

"Oh, my baby, my baby," said Viviana over and over as she hugged Francisco tightly.

"I got to go now."

Francisco pulled away from his mom. He reached out his hand to his dad, who gave Francisco a brief, odd look. Leaving so suddenly like this didn't make sense to the old man. Something was up. But Ernesto stayed quiet about his doubts and just reached out to shake Francisco's hand.

"Good luck" was all that he said. "Good luck."

PART TWO

SETON GROVE
ACADEMY

32

Are you ready to hear more?

Ready to peep the other side of this story? The antimatter to our story's matter? We're not in Harlem anymore. We're four hours north, up the Hudson River Valley, up in the sticks. If Harlem was the real world of kids from the streets, then this is the *surreal* world of kids with money. One of them had his house featured in an episode of MTV's *Teen Cribs*. Maybe you saw that episode; it's the one about the kid who had his entire bedroom built on a hydraulic platform that *rotated*—a full rotation every ten hours—so he could have a different view when he woke up each morning.

While Francisco's mother is back home bundling that God-given five hundred dollars into an envelope and stuffing it under her mattress—and, in an instant, doubling her life savings—up at Seton Grove, kids are getting five-hundred-dollar weekly allowances sent in the mail by their parents. World leaders send their sons and daughters to this school. The school is 99 percent rich kids and 1 percent scholarship kids. That 1 percent exists pretty much just so the school can say it supports diversity. *One percent.* It's like the reverse from the rest of America.

And you can imagine how that 1 percent can feel a bit awkward on campus.

For instance, have you ever watched nature shows about sharks, and you see the sharks swimming around with tiny fish latched onto the sharks' backs? That's pretty much what goes on at Seton Grove. The 99 percent are the sharks, and the 1 percent are, well, you got it—they're the scrawny little fish barely hanging on. What's interesting is that those little fish are actually using their mouths to keep the shark's skin healthy—they're literally licking it clean. It's the same way with how the 1 percent at Seton Grove keep the reputation of the school sparkling and clean.

The school loves to feature those 1 percent kids on its website and brochures for donors. Seton Grove *needs* its donors. Big-time. It's expensive for the academy to keep up its decorative lawns, its ivy-covered buildings, and its top-of-the-line gym.

And as long as we're talking about donors, then this is a good time to meet the sons of two of the school's biggest donors: Spencer St. John Jr., the son of a U.S. senator, and Anthony Chatterjee, the son of an Internet billionaire—two of the richest of the rich kids, and (as chance would have it) Francisco's roommates.

33

November 12

Spencer St. John Jr., a boy with more punctuation in his name than a sentence in Russian literature, was acting like a total jackass.

"Francisco!" he kept yelling across the room. "*Frrrancisco!*" rolling his *r* with a stupid mock-Latin accent.

Spencer laughed to himself and slurped soup from his Styrofoam cup of ramen noodles. Chicken teriyaki flavor. He sat back on his bed, which looked like an avalanche of clothes had fallen on it. In the bed next to him was Anthony Chatterjee, also slurping ramen noodles. Shrimp-flavored.

Spencer's looks matched his upper-class, New England pedigree: ice-blue eyes, blond hair worn long and swept straight back, and sharp features that gave his face the appearance of always angling down onto everyone else. Anthony's skin was two shades darker, given that his parents came from India, but with his Charleston khakis and silk ties featuring sailing and cricket, he was no less preppy.

This particular Monday afternoon, Spencer and Anthony were playing their favorite prep-school game: hazing the new kid.

"I knew he was dumb, but I guess he's deaf, too," Spencer said to Anthony, loud enough for Francisco to hear.

Slurp.

"What do you think he's doing back there?" Anthony asked.

Slurp.

"Jacking off."

There's no such thing as privacy in a triple. Everyone could hear the other kids' snores, smell the other kids' farts, and detect the minor movements under the sheets of a boy masturbating himself to sleep. These were normal things to boys who had gone to boarding school since ages as young as eleven. But for Francisco, who'd had his own room for all sixteen years of his life, except when Vincent was living in it, it was awful. On the first day of school, he rearranged his oversized furniture around the cramped room like a game of Tetris. First he moved his dresser next to his window, then he snuck his desk to fit perfectly behind it. It gave him a little fort he could disappear into—slip on some headphones and study by himself, far away from his annoying roommates, from their stupid jokes and disgusting ramen noodles.

Francisco had never gotten used to the smell of those prepackaged noodles that seemed to be the staple diet of every kid in the dorm. He never figured out why rich kids ate so cheaply. Even the sight of them made Francisco want to vomit.

Spencer tipped the ramen cup to his mouth and drank the

last of its contents. He crushed the cup into a ball and lofted it across the room. It landed perfectly behind Francisco's dresser.

"Two points," said Anthony, who was a bit of a brown-noser to Spencer, a top dog on campus. Handsome, witty, evil—he had everything going for him. Also, his senator dad's poll numbers were way up, which added to Spencer's stock on campus. Anthony hung on to Spencer's coattails with as much tenacity as he could. Anthony imagined that one day, years from now, Spencer's connections might help Anthony get a job at a good law firm, and this long-range goal kept him laughing hysterically at every one of Spencer's offensive jokes.

"That was a *three*-pointer," advised Spencer rather strictly. "Are you back there, Francisco?"

Francisco's head popped up from behind the dresser. He held the crushed, leaking noodle cup.

"What is this?" he demanded.

"We want to know where you went this weekend," said Spencer. "We wake up in the morning and you're here, then you go out and never come back."

"Home. I went home."

"For Veterans Day weekend? Nobody goes home on Veterans Day," said Anthony.

"Did you see your family?" asked Spencer.

"Of course."

"And how *are* Mr. and Mrs. Ortiz?"

"They're good."

"Still together, huh?" said Spencer, who cocked his head, asking in the most sincere way he could. "I'm so impressed. Good for them. I understand that's extremely unusual in your . . . demographic."

"My demographic?"

"Yeah. You know," said Spencer, trying to rephrase his words delicately before giving up. "Forget it."

"How about your homies?" asked Anthony, trying hard not to smile. "Did you see your *homies*?"

"Or did you do any *drive-bys*?"

The two boys laughed hysterically. It was hard for Francisco to even take their insults seriously.

"Oh, wait! Wait, wait! I know!" yelled Anthony. "You went home to carry out a *revenge killing*. Drug-related, gang-related type of thing?"

Francisco shook his head. "You guys are dumb, you know that? Really dumb." He pointed to the books piled on his desk. "And I'm trying to get smart. I have a test tomorrow."

Francisco dropped down into his seat, disappearing behind the dresser and going back to work. He heard his awful troll roommates snickering. Heard Anthony slurp out the rest of his ramen and crush the cup, then watched as it came sailing over onto his side of the room and landed on his bed. The boys laughed. Francisco saw a few drops of shrimp-flavored juice dribble onto his pillow.

"He was homesick, I bet," said Spencer. "The poor baby missed Mommy and Daddy."

Francisco hurried over to his pillow with a roll of toilet paper and sopped up the mess. Tomorrow, he would retake the trigonometry test. Sine, cosine . . . the math symbols looked like hieroglyphics to him. He'd been studying for hours, and it still made no sense to him. He worried that he wasn't going to do any better on the test the second time around. Francisco had been a star math student back at Alvarez, but at Seton Grove, he felt like he'd never taken a real math class in his life. That public school had taught him absolutely *nothing*.

Back at his desk, staring at his math text, Francisco cursed every last teacher he'd ever had. He blamed them for the problems he was having, but the one thing he couldn't blame them for was the epic feeling of loneliness raging through his heart like winds across a desert plain. He couldn't even blame Spencer and Anthony because, after all, those idiots were right about one thing: The reason Francisco went home *was* because of homesickness. He missed his mom's cooking, and he missed hanging out and watching TV with his dad. He missed sleeping in his own bed. But most of all, he missed Reignbow. He just couldn't get comfortable living by himself at the dorm. Its crappy food. Its crowded rooms. Its awful people.

November 18

Boarding school was full of traditions. Some were stupid and silly, toothpick-sized pirate flags waved by privileged teenagers who had no real stomach for rebellion. One tradition was held the last Friday of every month, when seniors wore their blazers inside out. They walked the halls with tags hanging off their backs and the inside seams showing like ragged ruffles. The boys winked and laughed when they passed one another in the halls, but Francisco didn't understand what was so funny about inside-out blazers. To him, it was just stupid.

Other traditions were old and rich and, well, full of tradition. Francisco liked these more, especially the Sunday night ritual of the 647 members of the student body dressing in semiformal attire and walking in a quiet procession across the quad to the old school chapel. The campus lawns were beautiful at night; they spread out among gentle hills, dipping and fading into the lush woods that surrounded the campus. Gravel paths, lit by gas lamps, stitched across great swaths of grass.

Chapel was a two-hundred-year-old tradition at Seton Grove, and for Francisco, Sunday nights felt like stepping onto a movie set. The ancient stone chapel loomed hauntingly in the distance, and the air was quiet in a way that Francisco never experienced in Harlem.

Inside the chapel, students crammed into tight rows of wooden pews. Boys on one side, girls on the other. Feet shuffled and lips whispered until a bearded man took to the grand marble podium at front and shushed everyone with the lift of his hand. He was the headmaster of the school, Mr. Roy McDonnell.

"Welcome to the nine thousand one hundred fifty-eighth Sunday night chapel," Mr. McDonnell began. "Thank you for the patience of your minds and the openness of your souls."

Of course, the term *chapel* was a bit of a misnomer. Years ago, chapel used to be a religious service where students bent their heads for hours on end, listening to prayers that felt more like punishments, as a fiery pastor begged the forgiveness of a Protestant God so that He might save them from a brimstone Hell. In the 1970s, though, the religious stuff went out the window, and chapel became a nondenominational gathering held mainly for making school announcements. One by one, deans and teachers took to the podium and talked about clubs opening up, test dates being moved, and sporting events that everyone was encouraged to attend.

It was the sporting announcements, delivered by gruff Coach Klasky, who looked awkward and sweaty in his short knit tie, that elicited a raucous reaction from the student body.

"We have Thanksgiving break coming up this weekend, but the following weekend is a big one for our sports teams. I expect everyone to come out and show their Crusader pride." He unfolded a piece of paper from his pocket and read it out loud. "I got JV squash playing home against Killens on Sunday at ten thirty, and varsity swimming away against Country Day School on Sunday at two. But the big one, of course, is varsity basketball playing Braintree on Saturday at one."

Kids whooped and cheered from their pews. Braintree was Seton Grove's biggest rival—it had been that way for over a hundred years—and any mention of the school got the Seton Grove students nearly frothing at the mouth.

"This is a home game, so I expect everyone to be there. Be loud and proud for your fellow Crusaders!"

More applause. Even the faculty applauded. Francisco clapped, too.

As the announcements finished up and chapel came to an end, the school chaplain was the last to the podium. A distinguished old geezer who had been at the school for over forty years, he was tall and hunched, with big-knuckled, vein-covered hands.

"Good evening, boys and girls," said the chaplain in his gentle voice. "Let us lower our heads in prayer."

Francisco lowered his head but he kept his eyes open, looking around at the other kids. Just about everyone in the chapel was white. This fact still amazed him. Before Seton Grove, he hadn't dealt with many white people. Now, he was surrounded by them.

There were four black kids sitting at the back of the chapel, scholarship kids like him. Francisco had met them briefly at the beginning of school. They were a shy, defeated-looking lot, hunched over their prayer books. One of them was chewing on the cuff of his suit, the sleeve of which came down to his fingers. The suit fit him like a blanket.

Francisco shut his eyes, and while the chaplain prayed for the school, Francisco prayed for himself: He prayed that he wouldn't become mean like his roommates or insecure like the other scholarship kids, those four poor ghosts on campus. He prayed that he would not change into an alien person on this alien campus, but, like he'd promised Reignbow, stay true to himself.

"Incomprehensible Creator," the chaplain droned on, "we beseech Thee to enlighten our understanding, and remove from us all darkness of sin and ignorance. Give us a diligent spirit, a desire for academic endeavors, and a capacity for retaining our lessons. Amen." Then the chaplain raised his head and, with more energy and volume in his voice, declared, "And let's beat the dickens out of Braintree next Saturday."

Amens and cheers went up from the student body as they stood and filed out of the pews. Francisco fell in with the crowd and was heading for the exit when he felt a hand grab his arm and pull him back. Francisco turned and found himself looking into the pinched eyes and bushy mustache of Dean John Archer.

Dean Archer was the house master of Baker Hall, the dormitory where Francisco lived. Archer lived with his family in a small house directly across the road from Baker. Living so close to the dorm allowed Archer to keep tabs—in other words, *spy*—on the Baker kids. He was prickly, prissy, and a pain-in-the-ass.

"Francisco," said Dean Archer in a voice that sounded as if

a camel had stood up and begun conversing, "do you have a few minutes to talk?"

"Uh. Sure."

"Good. Let's meet at the Baker sitting room at eight thirty, shall we?"

Francisco nodded. "Anything in particular?"

"Yes, you," said Archer, staring at Francisco with a kind of freaky glare.

"Me?"

"*You*."

Then he stared again. Dean Archer was the king of awkward conversations and strange silences.

"Okay, I'll be there. No problem," said Francisco, hoping that—in fact—there wasn't one.

35

The so-called sitting room of Baker Hall made Francisco nervous just being here. There were marble busts and glass lamps and framed pieces of art on the wall. In the corner of the room was a grand piano paneled with darkly lustrous maple. There was probably more money nailed and glued and hung up in this single room than the entire school budget had back in Spanish Harlem. The Alvarez High School fund-raisers that parents worked so hard to host, the pleas for donations to buy basic things like books and pens—they all seemed so tragically silly to him now. It made him feel embarrassed for his old school and how impossibly out of touch they were with how the better half lived.

"How would you rate your level of success at this school?" said Dean Archer, leaning back in a padded leather seat until it creaked for mercy.

"You mean, like, on a scale of one to ten?"

"That would do. What number do you think you are?"

Francisco paused. It was the kind of question that was impossible to get right. If Francisco gave too high a number, then he wasn't being honest. If he gave too low a number, then it was an admission that he wasn't trying hard enough.

"I'd say six?"

Archer gave a pitying smirk. "I'd say closer to a three. Don't you think *three* would be more accurate?"

Francisco said nothing.

"I want us to make a vow to be honest with ourselves, shall we?" said the dean. He opened a folder on his lap. "Now, you're getting a C in U.S. history, a D in math, a C in American literature." He scanned through the rest of the file. "I could go on. I have notes here from all of your teachers, who have contacted me out of concern for your academic performance. Do you understand the seriousness of this?"

Francisco nodded. "If your grades remain this low, you will lose your scholarship. You transferred to Seton Grove for your senior year, which I know is hard," said the dean, sounding more bored than sympathetic. "But we need to see some academic improvement from you."

"Okay. You know I'll try."

"Let me ask you a question, Francisco. Do you feel like you're fitting in?"

"Uh-huh."

"Uh-huh? What does 'uh-huh' mean?"

"It means yes."

"Then why did you go home over the long weekend? It's certainly not something the school encourages this early in the year."

Francisco couldn't lie. The dean barely believed the truth from him, so he'd never believe a lie. "I was homesick."

"Homesick?" The dean looked disappointed. "Well, I hope you're feeling better now. Are you feeling better?"

"Uh-huh."

"Uh-huh?"

"Yes."

"Good. Well, I'm happy we had this little talk. Now, go hit the books."

"Okay."

"And one more thing, Francisco."

"Yes?"

"Don't study so hard that you miss your sleep. Don't pull all-nighters like some kids do. You need your rest. We're going to need you to help win that ball game for us on Saturday. All right?"

Francisco was slack-jawed as Dean Archer closed his file and left the sitting room. Frozen in his chair, Francisco watched him cross the road and disappear into his house.

Finally, Francisco took a breath. A thought kept looping in his mind, a thought that he couldn't imagine was true—but he couldn't discount either. It explained what he was doing at this school. The only reason they'd accepted him in the first place.

Basketball.

Sports were the *other* reason that donors gave large sums of money to Seton Grove. Its winning sports teams. This trend was not a secret to Seton Grove administrators, who knew that whenever the school won championships, donations went up. It was even more effective than a picture of a black kid and white kid studying together in harmony. Slap a shot of a team holding a trophy onto the front of a fund-raising pamphlet, and people started writing checks.

I'm just a ringer, thought Francisco. *I'm nothing to these people but a stupid, C-student, basketball ringer.*

36

Francisco didn't go home for Thanksgiving break. He told his parents he had too much schoolwork to do, and once again he was out of step with the vacation plans of the rest of the student body. With everyone else far off campus having turkey dinners with their families at home, Francisco had the dorm to himself.

Sleeping in late and walking the empty dormitory halls in his bathrobe, like a king in an abandoned castle, he simply knew he couldn't go back home to face Reign and Vincent again—not now, not after how he left. The loneliness he felt was dampened by the relief of being far away from all their problems. He took extra-long showers in the mornings, knowing that no one was going to be screaming at him to hurry. He watched TV late into the night in the common room, and didn't have to negotiate with other kids about who had control of the remote. Some staff and teachers were still on campus through the break, so the commissary stayed open, but the dining hall was always pretty empty, and he sat at the giant circular tables by himself, eating in blessed peace and quiet.

For a few hours each day he did manage to get some studying in, but really, if Francisco thought about anything in particular, it was about the upcoming basketball game. He'd looked forward to plenty of games before, but he'd never felt this worked up, this passionate about going onto the court and proving himself.

But what exactly was he going to prove? Well, he'd give them what they wanted. It's like that old saying: If you can't beat them, join them. But he was going to beat them *by* joining them. They wanted ghetto ball? A ghetto player? Fine, then this was going to be *his* court, and they were dangerously out of their element.

The following Sunday, the campus filled up again with students, and the weekend after that, it seemed like half of them were sitting in the bleachers of the basketball court, screaming their heads off. It was the game of the year. Four large buses full of Braintree kids drove onto the Seton Grove campus, unloading rival fans who were immediately taunted by Seton Grove kids holding up signs that read SETON GROVE BELIEVES and GET BRAINTREE!

Inside the gym, the two teams jogged onto the court. Francisco kept his hood over his head, trying to block out the sounds of the air horns, the feet-stomping, and the mixture of screams and boos. Kids from both sides of the bleachers—Seton Grove and Braintree—pushed signs up over their heads, waving them in the air.

BRAIN-DAMAGE!

Francisco ignored it all.

The ref gathered the players at the center circle, tossed the ball high, and that's when Francisco exploded, leaping above everyone else. At the first tip of his finger on the ball, all he saw was red. Shoving, pressing, hammering—he was relentless against the Braintree kids. He caught one skinny kid in the face with an illegal elbow shot. Everyone up to the highest bleacher heard the *smack*, like a snare drum. The boy let out a lone, hollow cry, then fell. Coaches rushed over.

The school nurse examined his nose, and then nodded to the ref, meaning that the boy was okay to continue playing. With some toilet paper jammed up his nose, the Braintree player was helped to his feet by two other players, earning a standing ovation.

The ref pulled Francisco over to the side and gave him a stern warning. Francisco refused to even look at the ref, glaring up into the gymnasium lights, murder in his eyes. His own teammates looked across the court at him like he was crazy. The buzzer blew, and Francisco stormed wordlessly past the ref, leaping into the game full-throttle.

Francisco felt like a thug on the court, an outcast even to his own team. In fact, he played for no team. He played only to release the anger he felt deep inside. He pushed, shot, scored. He wasn't passing to anyone. As soon as he got the ball, he'd go for the score solo. He was playing against the other nine guys on the court.

With seconds left in the first half, and even with Seton Grove up 48 to 45, the Seton Grove fans started booing Francisco. His own players were yelling at him to pass the ball. Coach Klasky called a time-out and grabbed Francisco by his jersey, dragging him until they were nose to nose.

"What the hell're you doing out there?"

"Winning," said Francisco.

"Don't get smart with me. You play as a team or you don't play at all."

Francisco shrugged. The clock buzzed. The game resumed. Francisco started with the ball, bounced it a few times, looked left and right at his teammates up near the hoop, waving their arms at him, calling for him to pass. As the final seconds of the half ticked away, Francisco drove the ball himself, leapt up, and shot—but several Braintree players dove at him, knocking the ball into the stands. The buzzer sounded again, and the half was over. The noise in the gym was overwhelming. Half the Seton Grove students were cheering, because they were winning, and the other half were booing, because Francisco had refused to pass.

On the "away" side of the court, the Braintree coach gathered his players in a huddle and told them, "We need to get a handle on that boy. I want two, three players on him at every moment. He's playing rougher than us, so we need to play rough back. Got it? And if the ref comes down on you for it, I'll back you all the way to kingdom come. Now, get out there and win!"

In the second half, Francisco felt renewed pressure: The Braintree players were on him tight. Shoving their hands in his face, jamming their legs against his, trying to make him trip. It seemed like whenever he got the ball, half the Braintree players jumped on him. Francisco tried to shake them off and drove the top of his head into one kid's side. The kid absolutely fell apart, collapsing onto the paint with his limbs scattering like shards of glass.

The team manager ran onto the court as the downed kid rolled around moaning and groaning. The stands went quiet. Rivalry was one thing, but seeing such violence was another. The ref yanked Francisco by the arm and gave him his second warning. The school nurse, who was suddenly becoming very busy, examined the Braintree player, touching his side and asking him questions. He whimpered like a little kid and was eventually helped off the court and led straight into the locker room. The game was over for him.

The rest of the players paced the court, their heads down, waiting for the game to resume. As the Braintree replacement took off his sweats and ran out to the court and the ref brought out the basketball, one of the Braintree players—who was covering Francisco—leaned in close and whispered, "Don't you dare try that on me, Spic."

The ref's whistle blew. The players launched into action, all except for Francisco. He stood there, dumbfounded, unsure if he had heard right. Coach Klasky started yelling at Francisco to get into the game.

"Stop standing there! Come on!"

Klasky was red-faced, with spittle flying from his mouth, but Francisco couldn't hear him—couldn't hear anything. The world turned to slow motion. He gazed across the stands, and it seemed as if all the kids were yelling at him, barking like savage dogs. He felt nothing but hatred raining down from both sides. Then he looked back at the play and saw the Braintree player who'd called him a Spic jog past with a smile.

"What'd you say to me?" said Francisco.

The player just smiled again.

Francisco started to walk. He walked toward the kid, walked right past half a dozen players jostling for the ball. Francisco ignored everything and, without thinking, slugged the insulting player in the stomach. The player toppled fast, piling onto the floor into a tight ball.

Francisco couldn't believe how fast he went down. For a moment, he was uncertain why he'd been afraid of these prep school kids. The whole lot of them. They could make him feel poor, worthless, and unwelcome with just a glance. But look at this: One punch, and down they went, crumbling like they'd been made of nothing but ash.

Then the thought stopped there, interrupted by a crush of arms wrapping around him, pulling him away from the Braintree victim, shoving Francisco to the ground. The back of his head hit the court, and sparks flew across his eyes. The sparks were his dreams igniting, and blasting into smithereens.

37

While the Seton Grove fans were still celebrating in the bleachers and spilling out onto the court, the Braintree coach had already stormed into the locker room and submitted his formal complaint. The final scoreboard showed Seton Grove over Braintree, 89 to 85, but the complaint demanded that the ref cancel the victory due to Francisco's violent play. To allow Seton Grove to keep the victory, the coach argued, would be to validate and encourage the type of ugly play seen on the court today.

As the Braintree students loaded into their buses, a group of Seton Grove kids taunted them, pounding on the sides of the buses, yelling in protest of the complaint. Things were getting nasty.

At the same time, inside the locker room, far from the noise, Francisco held a bag of melting ice on top of his head. Droplets of cold water leaked down his face. He moved his hand under the bag and felt a large, tender bump. "Ow," he said to himself.

He could see through the window of the athletic office. Coach Klasky was arguing with the Braintree coach, with the ref between them physically holding them apart. The boy he'd punched was sitting meekly in a chair off to the side.

Eventually, the office door opened, and the three men and the wounded boy poured out in grim silence, heading over to Francisco. Francisco put the bag of ice to the side and sat up.

"Francisco . . . ," started Coach Klasky.

"Yes?"

"This boy's name is Duncan Minsley."

Francisco nodded awkwardly at the boy. The boy kept his head down. He cradled his belly.

"You owe Duncan an apology," said Coach Klasky.

Francisco paused. "Why?"

"Are you kidding me?" yelled Klasky. "It's the first step to settling this whole problem you caused!"

"*I* caused?"

"Yes! Because of the complaint! If we're sanctioned in the league, it'll be trouble for you, trouble for me, and trouble for our whole team. Easiest thing to do is to apologize and try to be done with it."

Francisco looked up at the faces looking down on him. They were nodding their heads in agreement with Coach Klasky, looking very annoyed.

"I'm sorry," muttered Francisco.

"Sorry for *what*?" said Coach Klasky.

"I'm sorry for hitting him."

"Who's 'him'?"

"Duncan."

The coaches nodded to each other, as if whatever negotiating had been going on, the treaty was now complete. The ref said, "I'll let you know my decision later today." Then he and the Braintree coach led Duncan away.

Francisco turned to Coach Klasky. "That's it?"

"Keep your head on your shoulders next time, okay? Hopefully he dismisses the complaint. Time will tell."

"But he called me a Spic," said Francisco.

The coach leveled his eyes at Francisco. "Don't tell me that's never happened before."

"It doesn't make it right."

"Listen, you played like a maniac. And you lost your temper. You ever heard the expression about sticks and stones?"

"But, Coach, he called me a racial slur. This wasn't some stupid 'mama' taunt."

"I don't want to hear it, Francisco. Let's just try to put this thing behind us, okay?"

Silence.

"I said, *'okay?'*"

"Okay."

Francisco needed to sleep off the headache. Huddled in his jacket, walking across campus, he felt colder than usual. The early December sky was shiny and pale. Francisco worried he had a concussion. He wasn't the neurotic type, but visions of doctors and probes and claustrophobic scanning machines danced in his head.

As Francisco hobbled into Baker Hall, his head pounded even worse. If he was gonna die of embarrassment, and maybe die for real, too, then the very least that God could do for him was to let it happen in solitude. Before going into his room, Francisco made a small prayer that Spencer and Anthony would be out. He could only imagine what *their* perspective on the game was.

He opened the door. *Relief.* It was empty. Francisco crashed onto his stiff, jail-grade mattress, rolled across the blankets until he was wrapped up tight, and immediately fell asleep.

When Francisco woke up hours later, hunger burned at his

stomach. It was a good sign, at least, that he didn't have a concussion.

He went to the student union, with a sea of students passing by him, laughing, chatting, eating. Trying to be anonymous, Francisco snuck to the food service bar and waited with his head down until he got to the head of the line.

"Um . . . a chicken burrito, please."

The student cook stared at him, grinning ear to ear.

"Burrito, please? Chicken."

"You got it, killer."

"Huh?"

"*Killer,*" said the kid, nodding knowingly. He turned around and got to work on Francisco's burrito.

Other kids in line were staring at Francisco, too. Staring . . . smiling . . . one kid flashed him a thumbs-up.

"Actually, just cancel that burrito, okay? I forgot my wallet."

Francisco felt weird. Or everyone else just seemed weird. Either way, he needed to get back in bed. Sleep this off.

"Dude," said the cook, "this one is on the house. Your money is no good here."

"What?"

"Where'd you learn to whale on a kid like that?"

"What?"

"You, like, *destroyed* him. He had no idea who he was messing with, right? Out of the blue—wham—you killed him."

"It wasn't out of the blue. He said something to me."

"Well, Braintree had no idea we had a thug on the team. Mess with us? Boom!"

All the other kids in line laughed. Francisco looked from one to the next. Were they kidding?

"Didn't you hear? The ref denied the complaint," said the cook. "The final score stays. We beat Braintree because of you. First time in five years. We reversed the curse!"

"We're, like, totally the ghetto school of the league!" said another kid in line. They high-fived each other. "We're Seton *Ghetto* now. Seton *Ghetto* Academy!" they chanted.

Francisco took his burrito and passed over to the cashier. When he reached for his wallet, the cashier shook his head no. Instead, the cashier offered Francisco a fist bump.

Francisco returned the bump.

The cashier blew it up.

Francisco walked out to the seating area and saw some kids applauding him. He made a waving gesture that immediately felt awkward, like he was waving from a parade car. Sitting down, he cut into his burrito as a few more kids approached and clapped him on the back, congratulating him on the win. But they especially congratulated him on the fight.

Francisco felt the warmth of a smile on his face. He couldn't shake it, this bit of fame. The only thing was, he wasn't sure if this was the beginning of a new acceptance on campus, or if it would all disappear by tomorrow.

By the next basketball game on the following Saturday, he got his answer.

39

December 8

There was a ruckus in the stands. Two campus security guards pushed past a crowd of students and made their way up the bleachers. The security guards had been alerted by a teacher that a prank was about to unfold—literally *unfold*. The guards huffed and puffed as they climbed the packed bleachers. At the top, a half dozen students were pulling a large, rolled-up banner out of a bag, racing to get it open.

On the court, the first half of the game was winding down. It was already a rout. Seton Grove was up by twenty points over Country Day School, a private school in western Massachusetts. Francisco was having the game of his life, scoring fifteen points in the last ten minutes. Every time he got the ball, the Country Day kids stepped away, letting him drive the basket and lay the ball right in.

"Shut him down! Shut him down for God's sake!" screamed the Country Day coach.

But no one shut him down. No one dared try. Whenever

Francisco got the ball, the Country kids traded worried glances and backed off.

"Why doesn't *he* come out here and get his head knocked off," one Country player whispered to another about their coach.

The buzzer blew. The half was over. The Seton Grove fans leapt to their feet, chanting Francisco's name. Up in the top of the bleachers, the prankster kids had finally gotten the banner out of their bag and were running it across the back of the gym. Eyes popped. Mouths fell open. Fingers pointed to the banner written in about a thousand-point font:

WELCOME TO SETON *GHETTO* ACADEMY— now screw y'all!

Campus security finally stumbled to the top and tore the banner down in a great show. Hundreds of students rang out with a chorus of boos. Headmaster McDonnell, in attendance at the game, ran over to the control board and turned on the microphone.

"Settle down, please. Settle down, everyone."

No one cared.

From center court, Francisco watched this drama play out above him. He walked over to the bench and put his sweatshirt on as students chanted, "We're Seton Ghetto Academy! Seton Ghetto Academy!" They flashed fake gang signs to one another. It was stupid, even embarrassing. But Francisco laughed hysterically, something he had not done since arriving at Seton Grove months ago.

Ten minutes later, the ref came out to center court and

blew the whistle. The second half was starting. Francisco took off his sweatshirt and jogged onto the court. Cheering rose up around him like flames from a volcano, and the students wouldn't quiet down. The ref held the ball, waiting for everyone to pipe down so the game could start. But when Francisco took a small bow, they only got louder. Kids dropped their pants around their butts, gangsta style.

Frustrated, the ref drew the two coaches together, had a quick meeting, then came out waving for all the fans to quiet down.

Eventually, they did. The teams met at center court. The ref put the ball into play. Francisco got control immediately. Up ahead of him was the basket. He drove toward it with all his speed. No one could catch him—he knew it. *He knew it.* The crowded field of kids were behind him, falling farther into the distance with every bounding step that he took. He didn't look back. Not once. He didn't need to. He'd never have to look back again. Ahead of him was everything he wanted in life. Francisco went for it. And nothing could stop him now.

December 15

Have you ever heard that question about the Button? The magical Button that, if you pushed it, would instantly pay you one million dollars. That's all you have to do: Push the button. One little click. A million bucks.

But there's a catch. The Button is wired halfway around the world to some poor fellow—some guy you've never met and never will meet. If you push the Button and get your money, that guy will suddenly drop dead. Gone. Maybe it will happen while he is walking across the street. His legs will fall out from beneath him, and there he'll be, lying on the ground with a bunch of strangers standing over him, wondering what just happened.

The question is, for a million bucks, would you push it?

How do you think the other guy would feel if you did?

Well, that's pretty much how Vincent was feeling. Actually, that's *exactly* how Vincent was feeling, as he lifted his head off a chunk of concrete that he'd used as a pillow last night. There was a black man in his forties looking down at Vincent. The man wore a tie and was holding a briefcase. Probably on his way to work.

"Are you okay?" said the black businessman.

"What?" asked Vincent, gathering his senses. He'd forgotten where he'd fallen asleep. That happens when you're homeless. He was lying in front of a Laundromat, on Malcolm X between 128th and 129th. "What'd you say?"

"Are. You. Okay?"

"Yeah."

"You don't look okay."

Vincent sat up. He rubbed the spot on the back of his head where the concrete pillow had pressed into it. "I'm *fine*."

"Son," said the black businessman, "I'm only trying to help. You don't have to get mad about it."

"If you tryin' to help, then you got a couple dollars I can borrow for some breakfast?"

The businessman sighed, reached into his wallet, and shoved over two dollars.

"This will get you something at McDonald's. You're too young to be on the streets, friend. Much too young."

Vincent snatched the bills. "Either help me or judge me, dude, but don't do both."

The businessman huffed and—muttering a "Merry Christmas"—walked away. A McDonald's across the street caught Vincent's eye. Once inside he cut the line and ordered a sausage McMuffin, eating it in one big bite as he walked away from the register. He asked a passing woman for the time—eight forty-five—and headed out the door. On his way to school.

That businessman had a good point, though, thought Vincent. He felt too young to be homeless. It would take a lifetime to unravel the problems he'd created in his sixteen short years on this planet. He felt a depression setting in, like a damp, awful coldness that he couldn't seem to shake.

While Francisco was off becoming a hero to white kids by *pretending* to be ghetto, Vincent was actually *being* ghetto. And the truth is, it's a lot more fun to play the part. You get to walk away from the consequences.

Shaking his head clear as he walked, the memories of what happened came back to Vincent. His mom had kicked him out five nights ago. Vincent spent the first two nights of homelessness sleeping on Jason's mom's couch. But after the second night, Jason's mom—who was not the nicest woman in the world to begin with—told Vincent that if he was going to keep sleeping there, she was going to charge rent. Vincent grabbed his coat and left. Jason watched his buddy leave, shrugging and looking embarrassed, but there was nothing he could do.

Vincent had no place to go but home again. *Bzzz. Bzzz.* Vincent's finger kept pushing the buzzer for his own apartment—17G—for about five minutes, but there was no answer. Trying to fend off the cold wind, he wrapped his thin pleather jacket tighter around him. When his mom kicked him out, this jacket was all he had on him.

Bzzzzzzzzzzzzz.

Finally, a woman who lived on his floor came out of the

building. Her name was LaVerne, and she was in a wheelchair. Her hands were too arthritic for her to hold the wheels anymore, so she pushed herself with her feet, shuffling all around the neighborhood backward, collecting cans on her lap.

"Hey, Vincent," said LaVerne. She had a disturbingly deep voice. So deep you could barely hear her. Years of smoking. She still smoked. Go figure.

"What you doing here?" she asked.

"Me? I live here."

"I know that! But I thought you and your mom was movin' out."

"What you mean?"

"Yesterday she left with a suitcase. Told me she was goin' to see her sister. In Florida. I thought—"

"What? Did she say when she was coming back?"

"No. But . . ."

"But what?"

"She had a lot of stuff. You know, like she was gonna be gone awhile."

Vincent's face went hot. "Did she leave a key with you or anything?"

"No. Why? What's going on?"

"She left me," he said, more to himself than to her. "She left." His mind raced with what it meant. He had no key. He had no home. And now *she* was gone, too. It made him wonder how bad of a person he must be that a person as terrible as his mom couldn't even stand him nomore.

"She abandoned you?"

Vincent nodded.

"Now, that ain't right one bit. Not one bit, Vincent."

"You *think*?"

His eyes narrowed. His lips pressed like a clamp. He turned on his heel and walked into the streets, where the only place he could rest without being accosted by cops or bums was in front of a Laundromat, and the only pillow he could find was a concrete block.

"What's the use?" he'd started muttering to himself recently. "What's the use?" His life didn't seem like his to control. Someone else had their finger on the Button.

Press it. Go ahead. But let's recalibrate the payoff first. You won't get a million dollars. You'll just get a trip to Florida. Or a diploma from a fancy boarding school. Or maybe all you'll get back is your couch with no loafer sleeping on it at night.

Would you still push it?

Let's do one more thing: Let's recalibrate the stakes. Let's say the person you hurt isn't a stranger on the other side of the world. Let's say you know him. You've known him your entire life. He's your best friend, he's your son's buddy from the 'hood, or he's even your own son.

Would you *still* push it? Would it be worth it?

Well, apparently, the answer was yes. And the answer was yes for a lot of people. It was yes for Francisco; it was yes for Jason's mom, and it was even yes for Vincent's own mom.

Vincent, the poor kid who'd had the Button pushed on him three times in a row, disappeared into the streets of Black Harlem, feeling like the most hated kid in the world.

December 21

He was starting to smell.

Hang on. Smell? No. Spoiled milk smells. Garlic smells.

Vincent *stank*.

All he had were the clothes on his back. The pair of underwear he wore was his only underwear in the world. Those socks on his feet were his only socks. He was still going to school every day. It provided him with his one and only meal: cafeteria lunch. What else was he going to do with himself all day? After adjusting to the cold and hunger, the thing that bothered him most about homelessness was the *boredom*.

In class, the other kids scooted their chairs away from him. He saw a moat around him. And on the other side of the moat, some freaked-out glares of sickened-looking girls. Their noses scrunched up. Laughter hanging at the edges of their lips.

Kids talked to him less. They started talking to each other more *about* him.

"He wearing that same shirt again today."

"He got so skinny."

"He got AIDS."

"He on crack, 'cause that's what happens when you on crack—you don't care."

"No, he just gone crazy stupid. He lost his mind."

Everyone had theories. No one cared to ask. Homelessness is a state of being, a state of statelessness, but it is also a state of mind. Vincent walked through the halls feeling like an alien. He sat in the back of the classroom scratching a rash on his leg.

Then came the first real snowfall of the winter. It was the last school day before Christmas break. The school bell rang and kids streamed into the streets. Big, beautiful flakes dropped fast and heavy. Fingers scraped a layer of snow off the concrete, formed it into balls, lofted them into the sky. Laughter. Joy. In another time—in another life—Vincent would have been in the middle of the action, grabbing girls' shirts and throwing snowballs down their backs.

But here and now, in this reality, when snowflakes landed on his eyelashes, he rubbed them away and found tears in his eyes.

Where am I going to sleep tonight?

That was all he could think about. The sidewalk wouldn't cut it. Vincent headed into the streets, his sneakers getting soaked in the slush, and his thin pleather jacket, zipped up to his chin, just not cutting it, either.

He did have one other option, of course: Viviana. She had taken him in so many times as a little kid. If Francisco was like a brother to him, then Viviana was like a mother. All he had to do was knock, and she'd open the door for him.

But as he stood on the street fighting off the wind and snow, he couldn't bring himself to head east to her building. He couldn't imagine facing her when he looked like this, smelled like this.

The situation was more than just embarrassing—it was humiliating.

And anyway, he felt guilty enough having messed up Francisco's life. Vincent was carrying around more baggage than a luggage handler at JFK Airport, and the last thing he wanted to do was drag all that baggage into Viviana's home. There was a line in the sand that you never crossed—you don't mess with someone's mom. Moms work hard enough; you don't bring them down with your own problems. You just don't. And even Vincent knew that much.

On 116th and Lenox Ave., there was a shelter. Vincent had heard about it, but always avoided it. You know what they say about shelters: People steal your stuff while you sleep. People rape you. People get killed in shelters. Shelters are *the last resort* for only the most desperate. So Vincent trudged on through the snow. Cold. Hungry. Tired.

Desperate.

Maybe it was the fact that there was no heat in Lily's apartment building. The first snowfall of the year brought an awful cold snap to the city. Batteries run weaker in the cold, and with Reignbow and her mom living in their parkas inside the apartment, the battery of Lily's electric wheelchair—which had been acting up for months—finally gave up.

The cold was also responsible for aggravating Lily's MS. Reignbow had never seen her mom so sick. Reignbow spent all her free time cooking, cleaning, and feeding her mom. As if Lily was a baby. The days of the Krew hanging out were a distant memory for her. Reignbow never saw any of them anymore. She hadn't heard anything from Francisco and assumed that he was either avoiding her for Christmas break or, more likely, staying up at school through the vacation. So instead of hanging out with her friends or her boyfriend, she was stuck at home watching a layer of ice form in a glass of water that she was drinking.

Lily called everyone she could think of: the wheelchair manufacturer, the battery installer, a friend of hers who owned the same wheelchair. She kept a shoe box in the closet full of receipts. *Flip flip flip.* She found the receipt for Scooter 123 and dialed the number on top of the receipt. After thirty minutes on the phone tree, pushing *1*, then *3*, then *9*, then *2*, but getting nowhere, Lily finally pressed *0* and held it until a voice came on.

"Yes, hello? This is Scooter 123."

"Is this a real human I'm talking to?"

"Real as they come. How may I help you?"

Lily explained the problem with her battery. The sound the motor made—*chunkchunkchunk*—whenever she tried to turn it on. "I think I need a new battery," she said. "I think it's still under warranty."

"That may be true," said the real live human, "but we don't handle warranties."

"Your company doesn't handle its own warranties?" Lily asked, sighing.

"No. You'll have to call the hospital who outfitted you with our wheelchair. Maybe someone there can help."

So Lily called the hospital, and *they* told her to call Medicare. She called Medicare, and they told her that replacing batteries was not their problem and to call the manufacturer. Reignbow sat on the bed beside her mother, listening to each call while filing her nails.

Eventually, Lily got back on the phone with Scooter 123 and demanded, argued, lectured. *Someone* was going to pay for her new battery.

That *someone*, the manufacturer informed her, would end up being Lily herself. She could try to get reimbursed by some government assistance agency, but that would take time.

"Honey," said Lily, "they're gonna make me buy the damn thing. They say it'll cost three hundred and fifty dollars. Can you believe it?"

"That's messed up, Mom."

Lily plopped her chin in her palm and thought for a moment. "Well," she said, "I'd say this finally counts as a rainy day."

Reignbow glanced out the window. "It's snowing."

"I mean *our* rainy day. Our rainy day box."

Reignbow stopped filing.

"Could you go get me the phone book in the kitchen?"

Reignbow froze solid. Dread hung from her mouth like drool.

"Ma, you know, I can just push you around myself. It's not such a big deal."

"Not when we go outside, you can't."

"I can do it."

"Through snow? Slush? Be serious."

"Well, I have a few extra pounds to lose. . . . It'd be a good workout."

"Reign. Would you cut it out? Go get me the phone book."

Reignbow got up and disappeared into the kitchen. Her head was spinning. She dug the phone book out of a cabinet drawer cluttered with pots and pans. She remembered being in this exact spot in the kitchen with Francisco when he'd lied to her and when he'd wrapped his lie in a big smooch. She wished he were back here right now, his arms around her, so that she could grab him by the throat and smack him across the face.

Nothing that happened after that point was much of a surprise. It played out pretty much as Reignbow feared. She walked into Lily's bedroom and saw her mom there with the tin can—painted with a rainbow—open on her lap. Lily was flustered, counting and recounting the money.

"Honey?" she said, her voice rising in a panic. "What happened to our money?"

Reignbow said nothing. Lily looked up.

"Reign-baby?"

And then Lily got it. Not everything, not the details, not exactly what happened. But as Reignbow stood there with tears in her eyes and terror on her face, Lily understood the gist of the situation. She opened up her arms. "Come here, baby. Come here and tell me everything."

Reignbow unloaded. All of it. The loan, the lie, the bail, the Krew falling apart, and Francisco being gone—for over a month now—without calling even once.

"He hasn't e-mailed? Nothing? Are you serious?"

"Yeah. . . ."

"Oh, Lord. Baby, I had no idea. But I understand what it's like to be in love. And I understand why you did it."

Reignbow let out a breath of relief. She'd been expecting worse: yelling, screaming, disownment. It happened all the time between parents and teenagers. You only need to peek your head out the door to hear it happening right now in any given apartment. But in apartment 14J, it was playing out differently. It was playing out with love and understanding.

"Reignbow, look at us. Two broke, lonely women sitting around feeling sorry for ourselves. But we don't have to be. We're better than this. *You're* better than this."

"I messed up."

"Yes, you messed up. Huge. But what you need to remember is that we're going to come out of this. We'll manage somehow."

"I'm just so mad. Mad at myself. Mad at Francisco. You can't believe it."

"It won't help to be mad at him, Reign. What will help is to move on with your life. Francisco's apparently moved on with his. I had no idea you two weren't talking all this time." Lily sucked in a deep breath and blew out the air with her cheeks puffed up big. "These things *suck*. Believe me, I know. But you gotta move on. Instead of doing what you're doing. Which is nothing. Except moping."

"Move on to what? What do I have?"

"You have so much! You're in the choir. You got good grades. I know it seems like your friends are everything, 'cause I used to think that, too. But the fact is, you grow up. You go your own separate ways. And when that happens, you know what you realize?"

"What?"

"That the thing you'll always have—and only will have—is your family."

Reignbow sneered. She couldn't stand it when Lily got all rah-rah about their family. There wasn't much of a family to speak of. No dad. A sister who moved out at seventeen to follow some guy. What was there to cheer about?

"How many times have I told you that I'm going to register so that you can go on *American Idol* and audition? Right?"

"Oh, please."

"I'm serious! And every time I say it, you're like, 'I'm not gonna do it! I'm not good enough!' But how do you know, Reignbow? How do you know you can't be one of them?"

Reignbow shrugged. "I just *know*."

"No you don't. I will be there for you, no matter what. I support you. I support you with whatever you desire. And you're gonna make it. You're gonna make it big. And I'm gonna be right there in the audience applauding you and loving every second of it."

Reignbow could feel her eyes starting to press out tears. There was nothing in the world sadder than impossible dreams. She used to dream at night about singing onstage, surrounded by tens of thousands of screaming people. Touring the world. But when she woke up in the mornings, she was in her own bed, in her own apartment, in old Spanish Harlem. It was a relief. It was a disappointment. It was confusing.

Outside the window, she watched cars swerve through the intersection that had the busted traffic light.

"Reignbow? Did you hear me?"

Reignbow gave her mom a small grin. "Yeah." Through all the disappointments in her mom's life, Lily still tried *so hard*.

"You believe me, right?" asked Lily.

"I'd like to," said Reignbow.

"Well, that's better than nothing, I guess. But Reign, there's one more thing."

"Yeah?"

"Francisco wronged us both. And I can't let that stand. We're out a lot of money, and that's gonna hurt us down the road. So here's my new rule: I don't want him in this house. Never again. I don't want to see him or talk to him. I want that boy out of our lives for good."

January 4

It's amazing how life goes like the tides. They're either on their way in or on their way out. There is no stability, no middle ground: When things are going against you, it's a full-on assault, and no matter what you try, nothing works. Gamblers call it a losing streak. Writers call it writer's block. Wall Street brokers call it a bear market. Some folks in Harlem call it . . . life. Just, life.

On the other hand, when things are going right . . . well, everything seems so easy. And that's how it was suddenly going for Francisco at Seton Grove Academy.

Click!

The teenage photographer pushed the button on his digital camera. He looked at the tiny LCD screen, grinned with a bit of pride, and turned the camera around to show Mackenzie.

"Wow!" Mackenzie said. "That looks amazing! Like he's flying over the hoop and not even trying!"

Mackenzie was looking at a close-up picture of Francisco

dunking the basketball. His head was above the hoop. Both hands were on the rim. There was even a big ol' grin on his face, mugging for the camera.

The move looked effortless, all right—because it *was* effortless. Francisco was standing on a stepladder, posing in mid-dunk.

"Get me a couple more and then we'll do the interview," said Mackenzie. The photographer nodded and snapped off a few as Francisco adjusted positions, leading with his left hand, leading with his right, sticking out his tongue Michael Jordon style, and then crossing his eyes and making a stupid expression.

Mackenzie laughed. "Great, great. Let's lose the ladder. Francisco, want to join me on the bleachers, and we'll do the interview?"

Francisco climbed down the ladder. He slapped hands with the teenage photographer. "That was a cool idea," said Francisco. "Inspired."

"Thanks, bro. Go, Crusaders," said the photographer. He folded up the ladder, and the clanking metal echoed high into the rafters of the empty basketball court. Francisco looked around this multimillion-dollar facility. When it was empty, you could really see how grand it was, how impressive that a *high school* should have such an amazing gym. It made him feel like he was playing NCAA ball right here.

Francisco followed Mackenzie up to the eighth row of the bleachers. Mackenzie Burton. Blond, thin, and unbelievably cute in a blue skirt and white-collared shirt. She was a junior, and the editor in chief of the student monthly newspaper, *The Crusader Minutes*. It was the paper that got delivered in shin-high piles to every corridor of every building on campus and pretty much stayed there untouched until the following month, when the piles were stuffed into recycling bins and new editions replaced them.

Mackenzie was writing a feature about Francisco, how he was leading the team to its best undefeated season in decades. And while it was true that the *Crusader Minutes* wasn't exactly *Sports Illustrated*, it was still pretty cool to have his picture on the cover of any magazine.

Sitting down on the bench, Mackenzie set her iPod in the space between them and pressed the Record icon.

"So," she said, "how do you feel about being Seton Grove's best player ever?"

Francisco laughed with a little embarrassment. "Good, good. I feel good when you put it that way."

"What would you say is the secret to your success?"

"Nothin'. I'm just doin' my thing. Ballin', you know?"

"*Balling?*"

"Yeah. Like, everyone else is out there *playing basketball*. But there's a difference from what I do. I ball. I learned what I do on the streets of Harlem."

"But it's the same game."

"The rules are the same. The objective is the same. Scoring baskets. But it's all in how you play it. You got to play it like you live your life. As if it matters. As if it's the most important thing in the world."

She couldn't help but grin.

"So how has the rest of the transition been?"

"What d'you mean?"

"You know, living in the dorm, eating our rotten cafeteria food."

"Not much to say on that front. The food sucks, but the kids are all right. Some of them, at least." He shrugged. "It's not really my crowd."

"Maybe they're intimidated by you."

"By me? That's crazy."

"No, it's not. After all, I'm sure you've heard the rumors swirling—"

"What rumors?"

"Well, given your background and everything, that you're in a gang."

"What?"

"It's what people are telling me. I'm surprised you haven't heard them."

"No. But I'd like to hear them now."

"They say that you were in jail. That a gun was found in your gym locker."

Francisco laughed openly. "I've never been in jail. And do you really think they'd allow an ex-con at this school?"

Mackenzie shrugged. "I'm just reporting what I hear."

"Well, none of it's true."

"But how about the part about being in a gang? Some say Crips, some say Bloods."

"I can't believe this is real."

"It's all everyone's talking about. A real gangbanger living on campus? C'mon. It's juicy."

"There's nothing juicy about it. It's just my life."

Mackenzie smiled. His earnestness was sweet.

"That's a good quote for the article," she said. "But you're kind of dodging the question."

"What question?"

"Crip or Blood?"

Francisco was becoming familiar with the tenacity of rumors. He could deny it. Right here. Right now. But what good would it do? Since day one, he'd been trying to push back on everyone's assumptions about him, to play the straight kid. All he'd gotten for his efforts was skepticism and disappointment.

Rumors were tenacious all right, but used correctly, they also had power. The gangsta image now seemed to be working for him. Getting interviewed for the student paper? By a pretty girl? C'mon.

"No comment," he said coyly.

"No comment?"

"No. Comment." It may have been a lie, but it was better to be a liar among friends than to be a saint all by himself.

Mackenzie touched the iPod screen and ended the recording. She turned her blue eyes up at him, held them there, two drops of rain heading right at him. Her intensity caught him off guard and he looked down at his feet.

"So, when does the article come out?" he said, breaking the awkward silence.

"I don't know. A few months probably."

"A few months!"

"Don't sound so disappointed. It's a free paper. You get what you pay for."

"I guess," he said, shrugging.

She lightly touched his knee. "It's gonna be a cool article, I promise."

He nodded and looked down at her hand. It didn't move.

"So I have another question," she said.

"Yeah?"

"Off the record, I'm just curious how it's been socially for you."

"Like . . . what do you mean?"

"Like, have you made, um, friends?"

"I pretty much hated everyone when I first got here. I'm not sure I like them much now, but at least they're being nicer to me. At least, ever since this basketball insanity took off."

"So . . . friends."

"Let's just say that I don't think I'm going to be keeping in touch with anyone after I graduate."

"Not like you are with your old friends at home, huh?"

"Well, I'm not sure they want to stay in touch with me any-more."

"Sounds lonely."

"I don't know. . . . A little bit, maybe. But things are better at school now. So I'm happy about that."

"We-e-e-ll," said Mackenzie, "if you want, we can be friends."

Francisco felt himself blush. Her eyes lingered on him. Unless he was reading her wrong, here was a blond white girl coming on to him.

"That's nice," he said slowly.

"Yeah?"

"But the thing is, I have this girl back home."

"Oh."

"And I got a lot of making up to do to her." He was almost kicking himself for turning Mackenzie down, but it was the only thing he could really do. It was Reign he was thinking about, not himself.

Mackenzie pocketed her iPod and stood up.

"That's okay," she said. "But just know that it's hard to keep up relationships back home. Life changes once you're at school. Take it from me, long-distance romances almost never work out."

Francisco nodded. "That's true. But I don't think you and me being friends is going to help my odds very much."

February 16

One sock.

One shoe.

Why anyone would steal *one* sock and *one* shoe was beyond Vincent, but that's what he discovered when he woke up in the shelter and planted his feet on the floor. One of his feet was naked. Maybe the thief only had a right leg? He glanced around the shelter at the two dozen other cots where folks were waking up, packing bags, heading in and out of the very busy bathroom. None of them looked like a thief. Or rather, maybe all of them looked like thieves, but none looked like *his* thief. The whole situation would have been funny if it hadn't left him in such dire straits. After all, it was winter. You need your socks and shoes in the winter. Especially when you're living in the streets.

One trash bag.

One tissue box.

These were the things that Vincent was now wearing on

his right foot. The bag was wrapped around his foot and held in place by a rubber band. Then he slipped his bag foot into a tissue box he found in the Dumpster, and off he went. Sloshing through the snow.

There was no way he could go back to school now. Smelling bad was one thing, but showing up with a trash bag for a shoe? No way.

He hadn't seen Jason in almost two months. Jason had spent the entire New Year's break sitting on his couch at home, watching Disney XD, eating Doritos and ice cream. Without Francisco, there was no Krew, and without the Krew, Jason got depressed, getting fatter and fatter every day. Vincent never saw Boonsie, either. She spent all her free time after school working on college applications. Dinky was off the map, too, spending her time with her basketball friends. She wasn't as close to them as she was to the Krew, but at least they didn't fight with each other like the Krew did. At least they weren't falling apart.

Knowing Vincent, he should have been saddest of all about the Krew's demise, but in fact, he barely had time to think about it. There were bigger problems consuming him—like finding a safe place to sleep at night. No more shelters for him. He was gonna *keep* his left sock and left shoe, or die trying, so help him God. Actually, he didn't quite need God. All he needed was Jesus.

Jesus was a dude he knew. Well, it was really a dude his mom used to know. He was a dreadlocked dude who wore a hemp poncho and went by the name of Baby Jesus. Not Baby *He-zus*. Baby *Gee-zus*. He sort of looked like a baby because he was short and had a chubby baby face. And he kind of looked like Jesus, because he had this thick brown beard and long hair. It seemed sacrilege to actually call him by his nickname, because while we're all sinners, there were few sinners who sinned as badly as Baby Jesus.

Vincent's mom knew Baby Jesus because he did some pimping work in Harlem. Vincent's mom sometimes worked for him as a prostitute. Ugly, but true. When Vincent was a kid, his mom used to bring him around a motel, the Quality Stay on 144th, where Baby Jesus ran his business. Vincent was only five or six at the time, but he understood what he was seeing; he understood what it meant when Baby Jesus sent Vincent's mom into one of the motel rooms with a john. Vincent used to wait in the lobby of the Quality Stay for his mom to finish. Baby Jesus sort of took care of him, giving him a comic book to read till his mom came out, took a few bills from Baby Jesus, and headed home with her son.

Ten years later, as a sixteen-year-old, Vincent stood outside of the Quality Stay. It was a one-floor, cinder-block joint, painted all white and looking nothing like the rest of the four- and five-story brick buildings in Harlem. There were no windows on the building. Have you ever seen a place with *no windows*? Makes it look evil.

When Vincent walked into the lobby, the first thing he saw was Baby Jesus picking his teeth. After ten long years, he looked exactly the same. Same beard. Same hemp poncho.

Baby Jesus looked bored, too. As if he'd been sitting there all day. That's the thing about street life that no one ever talks about—the thing they never show in the movies. How boring it is. Pimpin', hookin', hustlin', dealin'—they always seem so exciting in the movies. Set to a thumping hip-hop soundtrack. Paranoia and danger lurking around every corner. But it's not like that in real life. Most of the time, street life amounts to sitting on a park bench somewhere, waiting for the action to come to you.

Near one of the rooms, Vincent spotted two black women with tiny compacts, reapplying their makeup. They had platinum hair, rainbow leggings, and such sad, damaged eyes that Vincent had to look away quickly.

"Can I help you?" asked Baby Jesus.

"I . . . I used to know you."

"You did?"

"Yeah. My moms. Beverly. She used to, uh, work here."

"Beverly, Beverly, Beverly," Baby Jesus said to himself, trying to jog his memory. "Yeah, I think I remember her. You was that boy of hers, right?"

"Right."

"So what's going on? She interested in working again? I'll find a spot for her in the rotation no problem."

"No, no. It's nothing like that. See, she's gone. Moved away from the city. And I was wondering, if there was any way . . ." Vincent felt himself getting really emotional. The waterworks were coming, he could feel it. Up till now, he'd felt nothing but anger over everything that had happened to him. But saying it out loud, it hit him how truly sad his life had become.

Baby Jesus held up his hand. "Stop right there, little brother. I see what you're going through. I see you got a bag on your foot for a shoe. You need some help."

"Yeah."

"You was a smart child, little brother. I remember that. It's a shame you wound up this way, but I understand. You can't help life. So, listen, here's what I can do for you. I can give you a little bit of food, all right? And I can give you a place to sleep at night. If a room's free, you can have the room. If not, then this lobby is all yours. It ain't much, but it ain't the streets."

Vincent shook his head in disbelief. "Thank you, all right? I'm grateful."

"But listen, little brother, in exchange, you got to do something for me."

"Like what?"

"It ain't much. Sometimes I get these errands and shit that come up. Maybe you can go run those errands for me? It'll earn your keep here and put a few dollars in your pocket. Sound good?"

"Sounds good to me."

Baby Jesus reached over and shook Vincent's hand.

"So we have a deal?" said Baby Jesus.

"Yeah. Deal. But what kind of errands we talkin' about?"

Baby Jesus busted out laughing. It was funny how someone as street smart as Vincent could still be so naive.

The jobs were simple. Take a brown bag and bring it to an address; trade the bag for a wad of cash; be back at the hotel in twenty minutes. The first few times he did it, Vincent snuck a peek inside the paper bags. Sometimes it was pot, sometimes 'shrooms. Sometimes a baggie of cocaine. They were all small jobs, a few ounces here or there delivered around the neighborhood. Baby Jesus was not a big-time dealer, although he certainly had ambitions to be.

Every few weeks, Baby Jesus would slip Vincent a hundred dollars. Just like he'd promised. Baby Jesus proved to be a man of his word. At nights, if the rooms were booked, Baby Jesus laid a sheet of cardboard on the lobby floor, and Vincent curled up and slept on it. No one ever bothered him. No one . . . until one night.

The skies had dumped a foot of snow over Manhattan. Across the city, kids were opening their mouths and catching flakes on their tongues; lovers traipsed through Midtown gazing up at the beautiful white wonderland.

But uptown in Harlem, Vincent was shivering on the concrete floor of a flea-bag hotel. His cardboard sheet was soaking wet from the slush tracked in by the shoes of johns and hookers walking in at all hours. He was in a state of half sleep, when suddenly a burst of heat shot through his head. Like an electrical bolt.

"Good morning, sunshine!"

Vincent opened his eyes to the sole of a Timberland hovering above his face. "Remember me?" Peering behind the boot was RJ. The thug had a big ol' grin. "Maybe this'll jog your memory."

He stomped down, and Vincent rolled over, cradling his face, scuttling against the wall and waving his arms in surrender. "Yo, yo—stop it! *Please!*"

Standing next to RJ was a guy named Grind. Grind was even bigger, more muscled than RJ. The lower down the ranks the muscle went, the bigger these guys got.

"We stop when you pay us Boom's money," RJ said.

"What?"

Crack! Another bolt of electricity through his head. Another reminder.

"Grind here gonna check your pockets, Vincent," said RJ. "He find nothing, then you a dead man."

RJ pulled out a gun and pointed it at Vincent's head. He pressed the tip of the barrel hard enough that it left a deep red circle between Vincent's eyes. Vincent didn't move an inch as he felt Grind's big hands plunge into his pockets—pants, coat, shirt.

"This looks bad," said RJ. "It looks like maybe you broke."

Finally, Grind found something.

"Lookee this," said Grind. His hand emerged with a snaggle of twenties and fives. RJ counted the bills.

"Got almost eighty bones here."

"Now, this here's what you would describe as a *judgment call*," said RJ, thinking deeply. "But I think this eighty might be enough to buy you your life—for a short period of time. You lucky, Vincent. You gonna get another chance." RJ slammed his boot into Vincent's ribs. "But next time, you better have it all."

The two thugs walked out. Vincent tried to sit up, but everything hurt too much.

He heard a prostitute enter the front door and clear her throat. "What happened to you?" The way she said *you*, it sounded more like she was accusing him of something, rather than being worried about him.

"I think I need a hospital," Vincent managed to whisper. "Could you call for help?"

The prostitute did nothing. She kept staring at Vincent. "You got yourself mangled, boy."

"Could you call?" he whispered again. "Please call."

The prostitute sighed like it was a lot of trouble for her, pulled out her cell phone, and dialed.

March 16

It was the most interesting thing Anthony had read in months. It was certainly the most interesting issue that the *Crusader Minutes* had published in years. When he got to the last line of the exposé—Francisco's coy "no comment"—Anthony smashed the paper shut and yelled out, "Tell the truth!"

Francisco, who was hidden behind his dresser, curled up in bed with his American history text, said, "About what?"

"About what Mackenzie asked you. About the gang. Your gang affiliation."

"Like I said, no comment."

"Why not?"

Francisco poked his head above the dresser. " 'Cause they kill you if you tell."

Anthony's eyes lit up. "*Who* kills you?"

"Forget it. I've said too much already." He dove behind the dresser and disappeared into his book. Quiet suffocated the room like a gas. The curiosity was killing Anthony.

"Listen, I get it, Francisco. You don't trust me. I know I haven't exactly been the best roommate in the world." There was no response from Francisco. "But living in a dorm is hard. All these kids crammed on the same floor? The constant noise? The competition over grades, colleges? It's crazy stressful! Things get out of hand . . . and *I* got out of hand."

After another moment of silence, Francisco mumbled, "So?"

"So I'm apologizing for being a terrible roommate. I want to be friends."

"Why? 'Cause I'm famous? *Now* you want to be friends?"

Anthony sighed. "I deserve that."

"Yes you do."

"Um, Francisco?"

"Yeah?"

"Could you come out from there? It's weird talking to your dresser."

Francisco poked up again. "You and Spencer have made my life hell."

"I know, I know. But it was hell for me, too."

"What did *I* ever do to you?"

"Nothing. It wasn't you. It was the rest of the school. I used to get harassed every day for just rooming with you."

"Me?"

"Yeah. They said I drew the short straw, getting stuck with a kid from the ghetto. Said I should lock up my belongings every night."

"Well, screw everyone."

"Easier said than done. I put up with a lot defending your name!"

"You *defended* me?" said Francisco, his words boiling in a pot of skepticism. "When?"

"Oh, all the time."

"Yeah, right."

Anthony scratched his head. "Tell me something: What's the one thing you hate most about living in the dorm?"

"Besides you?"

"Seriously."

"The showers. I'm the new kid and I have no seniority, even though I'm a senior. I hafta wait in the shower line with the freshmen. It sucks."

"All right, then you can have my dibs on the shower. I'll take your spot with the freshmen. For the rest of the year."

"For real?"

"For real."

"Okay. Thanks." Francisco dove back behind his dresser. Then he thought for a moment, and reappeared. "And I hate how crowded this room is."

"No problem. Push your dresser this way. I'll give you, say, 40 or 45 percent of the room. We'll measure it. It's not like I need any room, really."

Francisco smiled. "Cool."

"See? This is what I'm talking about," said Anthony, tapping his fist to his chest twice. "Respect."

"Did . . . did you just get gangsta on me, Anthony?"

"I did," he said. "So please, give me a little something in return. Some inside knowledge about the gang."

"You've been Spencer's boy all year. Sucking up to him. Now you're sucking up to me. You don't think I see that?"

"So what?" said Anthony, shrugging. "I know I'm a suck-up. I'm great at it, too. But Spencer is old news. Who cares about who his dad is when there's an actual basketball star slash gang member living on campus? Do you know how cool that makes you? I need that coolness to rub off on me." Anthony rubbed his face. "Come on. Rub off on me, Francisco."

Francisco had to clench his jaw not to laugh out loud. He tucked his smile into his palm, pretending to scratch his nose. "Okay," he said. "This isn't something that I can just go around yapping about with anyone. My secrets come with a risk."

Anthony nearly shouted with excitement. "I'm willing to take that risk! Damn, I swear I won't tell a soul. But if everyone in school just *knows* that I know about what gang you're in . . ." Anthony looked up at the ceiling, dreaming. "I'll be the second-coolest kid on campus. Second to you, of course."

Francisco came around the dresser and sat on Anthony's bed. He spoke in a quiet, yet clear voice. "The truth is, Bloods and Crips are dinosaurs. They've become irrelevant on the streets. I'm in a different gang altogether."

"Seriously?"

"Seriously. This new gang is taking over those gangs. Blood on the streets. True story."

Anthony slapped the *Crusader Minutes*, tearing a hole in the paper. "Ha! I knew it! I knew you were the real deal! You've been sitting there quiet, keeping to yourself, but I've had my eye on you, Francisco. I knew you had an awesome secret."

"Yeah, you knew. Congratulations," said Francisco flatly. "Anyway, the gang I'm in . . . we called the Kaos Krew. With

K's, not *C*'s." Francisco intentionally dropped the verb in his sentence. He figured it would make him sound more authentic.

"Holy shit!" yelled Anthony. "That's incredible!"

"In fact," said Francisco, "I been thinking of starting a chapter of the Kaos Krew around here. Kaos Krew: Upstate. What you think?"

"I think it sounds *amazing*."

"So there you go." Francisco leaned back with satisfaction. "Now you know the truth."

And the truth sank in. Anthony gulped down a nervous breath. "Francisco?"

"Yeah?"

"I want in."

"In what?"

"The gang. I want to join. I want you to make me a gang-banger."

But this time Francisco couldn't hold in the laughter. It tore out of his belly, roaring down the halls, and didn't stop for a full minute.

"What the hell's going on in here!" yelled Spencer, watching from the doorway as Anthony and Francisco scooted Francisco's dresser into Spencer's side of the room. "Stop that right now!"

"We rearranging," said Anthony, skipping the *are*.

"Not in my part of the room, you're not. And why are you talking that way? What were you guys laughing at? I could hear it all the way down the hall."

"So?"

"So why were you laughing!"

"It was nothing," said Francisco.

"It *sounded* like something," said Spencer, who couldn't bear to not be in on a joke.

"You're never going to believe it," bragged Anthony. "Francisco is starting a gang on campus. A real inner-city gang. And I'm totally in it."

"Bullshit," said Spencer. "You're so gullible, Anthony."

"No I'm not."

"Yeah you are. You believed that article? *No comment?*" He glared at Francisco. "You meant to say *no idea*." Spencer threw his book bag onto his desk. After shoving the dresser back to its original spot, he sat down, switched on his desk lamp, and started pulling out books.

"You're wrong, Spencer," said Anthony.

"There's no gang. Believe me," said Spencer.

"How would you know?"

"Because first he acts like he's a nobody. Doesn't look at us. Doesn't talk to us. But then he starts to get a reputation, and suddenly he spouts off like some kind of gangsta idiot. But the fact is, he has about as much connection to the gang world as I do."

"Prove you're right," said Anthony.

"Okay, I will." Spencer turned to Francisco and addressed him with a tone of cross-examination. "If I wanted to, could I buy drugs from you?"

"What?"

"Pot. Or even cocaine. I mean, if you're a gangster, then you must have drug connections, right?"

"Sure."

"So let's put our money where our mouths are. You say you have gang connections. You claim, therefore, that you have access to drugs. So if I asked, could I buy drugs from you? Could you be my drug dealer? What do you say?"

"I'd say that you're bluffing," said Francisco.

"Try me."

Spencer grinned, a hunter with a deer in his crosshairs.

"Shut up, man," said Anthony, swatting Spencer in the arm.

"Drugs are something different. We're not even talking about drugs."

"I never touch that stuff anyway," said Francisco. "Believe me, if I had, I wouldn't be at this school."

"Oh, seeing the way you play on the court, I have a feeling that you'd be a student here no matter what." Spencer smirked. He turned away and opened a book. Francisco stood there like a bump on a log. Bested by Spencer, once again.

Just then, there was a knock on the door. A freshman poked his head in.

"Francisco?" said the freshman. The kid had red hair, big ears, and was appropriately nervous poking his head into a senior's room.

"Yeah?"

"There's a phone call for you downstairs. On the house phone."

"The house phone?"

"Yes."

"They say who it is?"

"Some kid named Jason."

"Jason?"

"Yo, what's up, F?"

"What's going on?"

"I been trying to call you on your cell, but I couldn't get through."

"Uh, yeah. It's broke or something. What's good, Jase?"

"There's been an emergency. It's V."

"It's *always* an emergency with Vincent."

"No, but it's different this time. I just pulled Vincent out of the hospital. He got three broken ribs. A concussion."

"What happened?"

"Boom sent two guys after him. I can't believe I'm even saying it—they almost *killed* him."

Francisco covered the receiver with his hand. The "house phone" was a pay phone in the lobby of the dorm. It was a busy area and a bad place to have a personal conversation. Students passed by left and right.

"You serious, Jase?" he whispered.

"Yeah. It doesn't seem real. Until you look at Vincent. Then you know it is. He all fucked up. This situation is serious."

"I don't know what to say, Jason."

"You don't?" said Jason, his voice rising.

"No. I don't even know what to do."

"That's why I'm calling. He needs your help."

"*My* help? I couldn't help that kid when I was down there. I definitely can't help him now."

"So that's it, then? You just gonna let him hang for this?"

"No, but what can I do? What the hell am I supposed to do from all the way up here?"

"I don't know! Something! You were always his boy, F. Plus, it's that five hundred you got him wrapped up in that's causing the problem. Boy felt like he owed."

"That boy needed to follow my directions better. I was doing *him* the favor. He got to act like a man about it."

"That's cold, F. His face, you should see it. It's all busted up. Looks like he fell off the Empire State Building."

Francisco got quiet for a while, listening to the background hum of the phone line. It was hypnotic, almost relaxing. "Yo."

"Uh-huh?"

"Yo, Jase?"

"Yeah?"

"I just got to say something first. I got to say . . . it's good to hear your voice. I mean it."

"Yeah. Yours too."

"I was worried I was never going to hear from the Krew

again. . . . But at the same time, I was *scared* to hear from one of you. Of what you might say to me. But it's nice right now. It's nice to be reminded."

"Of what?"

"Of what it felt like to have friends."

"Okay, F, that's all fine 'n' shit. But we got serious problems to figure out. I ain't just gonna hang up the phone and let this slide. Let Vincent die. Not until we have ourselves a good plan."

Francisco shook his head. "It ain't never gonna end, is it, Jase?"

"Well, Boom ain't never gonna stop. I promise you that."

"How much does Vincent owe now?"

"Around six hundred for sure. I don't exactly know. He hiding out uptown, doing small jobs for Baby Jesus. Living in the fucking lobby of a motel. Shit's depressing, man."

Francisco had heard of Baby Jesus, and knew some people who regularly bought from him. The dude sounded like a creep.

"Listen, you just tell Vincent to hang tight."

"True story?"

"True story. Tell him to hang tight. I got a plan to get this all squared away."

"What is it?"

"I can't say yet. I got someone to talk to up here first. But I'll call you in a couple days."

"Don't forget us down here, F."

"I won't."

"I'll hear from you? You sure?"

"Yes. I promise. Just give me some time."

"Ai'ight."

"All right."

Click.

April 20

Vincent was his own worst enemy. Francisco knew that, and so did Baby Jesus. That's why Vincent was kept in the dark about *everything*. All he was told was that he was going to be making a delivery. No one would tell him more than that.

In the Quality Stay lobby, Baby Jesus handed Vincent two things: a round-trip ticket on Metro-North, and a large paper bag full of groceries.

"I need you to deliver this today," explained Baby Jesus. "It's extremely important."

Vincent looked inside the bag. "What is this?" He pushed aside a carton of rice, some milk, cans of beans and vegetables, and a box of breakfast cereal. "There's nothing in here."

"Yeah there is."

"What?"

"Groceries."

"This a joke?" said Vincent, looking into Baby Jesus's eyes, which revealed nothing.

"Groceries ain't much of a joke."

"No doubt."

"Do you find groceries funny?"

"No."

"All right, so now that we got any laughter outta the way," said Baby Jesus, serious as a straight line, "should we get back to business?"

"Sure."

"Then take this."

Baby Jesus handed Vincent the Metro-North ticket.

"You'll be taking the eight forty-seven this morning. Don't be late. Got it?"

"Yeah."

"You'll take it up to Coldwater. It's a four-hour ride. Understand?"

"Milk's gonna spoil. There's milk in here."

"You're not paying attention, Vincent."

"Yes I am."

"What stop are you gettin' off?"

"Coldwater."

"Good. To hell with the milk. You'll exit out the rear of the train. You'll wait on the platform for ten minutes. *Ten minutes.* You follow?"

"Yeah. Ten minutes. Easy."

"At that point, your contact will meet you on the platform. You hand him the bag of groceries. He hands you an envelope."

"How do I know who the contact is?"

"You'll know."

"Yeah, but how?"

"I said you'll know! Stop asking me! Now, once you have the envelope, you get on the next train returning to New York. That train'll come thirteen minutes later. You use the other half of that round-trip ticket." Baby Jesus pointed to the ticket again. "And you come directly here. You give me the envelope. At that point, I'll pay you for the delivery. Six hundred dollars."

"Six hundred dollars! Just for delivering a bag of groceries?"

"Yes."

"Groceries."

"They sure look like groceries to me. We back to that again?"

"No, no."

"Good. And one more thing."

"What?" said Vincent.

"What you got under that jacket?"

"A T-shirt."

Baby Jesus studied him up and down, like a fashion designer assessing an outfit. "Take the jacket off."

"Why?"

"Just give it to me."

Vincent did. It hurt his ribs to take it off. They still hurt from the beating. He winced several times. Then he felt naked and cold standing in just his T-shirt. It was freezing outside.

"*Now* you're ready to go," said Baby Jesus.

"But what about my jacket? It's cold and shit."

"You'll only be needing a T-shirt."

"Why?"

"For cover."

"Cover?"

"Yes. Cover. Now hurry. Your train's leaving soon, and you got a long ride ahead of you. Pretty ride, too. Make sure you look out the window. Smell the roses and shit."

It *was* pretty. The tracks brought the train up close to the Hudson River, where Vincent could see rowboats listing in the current, and tiny islands where some old wooden footbridges had been built and then collapsed decades ago. Beyond the river, the trees and the hilltops danced with one another, the trees overtaking the hills, and then the hills rising above the trees, back and forth in a gentle duet.

After months of sleeping on a piece of cardboard, his upholstered seat on the Metro-North train felt positively luxurious to Vincent. He worried about falling asleep and missing his stop, so he kept getting up and pacing the aisles. This behavior only served to worry the other passengers, who were already put off by his smell, that wild look in his eyes that marked him as homeless, and his sunken cheeks from not eating right.

When Vincent finally got off at Coldwater, he had no idea where he was. Pretty far north of the city, that was all he knew. What state was he in? New York? Connecticut? Massachusetts?

Vincent waited on the train platform with his bag of groceries between his feet, shivering in his T-shirt. He couldn't imagine who he was supposed to meet all the way up here. Only one other person had gotten off the train with him—a woman in a business suit—and she was long gone by now. The parking lot across the tracks was empty. Nothing but forest around him and the Hudson River behind him. Through the trees, he could see a couple of winding roads that led to some kind of college-campus-looking place maybe a mile away.

Ten minutes, huh?

Ten turned into twenty. His return train came and went.

Where is that fool?

Vincent worried that he'd gotten off at the wrong stop. He looked out at the Hudson River slipping by, rubbing his arms vigorously to get a little bit of warmth into them. It dawned on him that this was connected to the same river—a hundred miles south of here—that ran past his very own neighborhood. The river that ran beneath his and Francisco's pier. Down in Harlem, the river was full of trash and oil slicks. But up here, it was clean and gorgeous. Birds swam on the surface, picking at the ripples fish left behind.

Man, he thought, *how could it all be connected?*

Harlem might be the center of the world, but it wasn't nice like it was here. Here, the ground was clean. The roads were quiet. The air smelled fresh.

Vincent had no idea there was anything worthwhile in the world outside of Harlem. . . . But then he saw this place.

And this place ain't too bad at all.

52

"Hey, punk! Get the hell out of here before I call the cops!"

Vincent whipped around and couldn't believe his eyes. Francisco stood at the platform edge, laughing.

Vincent went over and hugged his best friend. Francisco saw a dull yellow bruise on Vincent's face. "Son of a bitch."

"Forget that—yo, what in the world are you doing here?" asked Vincent.

"Well, welcome, V. Welcome to my home."

"You live here? This is your school?"

"Yeah. Over there."

Francisco pointed through the woods to the place that looked like a college campus.

Vincent whistled, impressed. "No wonder you don't come home nomore."

"So," said Francisco, quick to change the subject, "you brought the shit with you?"

"The groceries?"

"Yeah, dude."

"They're for *you?*"

"No. For someone else. I just arranged it."

"You arranged a drug deal?" Vincent wasn't sure why, but he felt disappointment in Francisco. It was hard to believe he was talking to the same guy he always used to know. "Why?"

"For you, idiot."

"Me?"

"Yeah, to make you some cash. There's a big drug purchase going on at my school. I got into it to make sure you get a piece of the pie, so you can pay back Boom. And be done with that dude once and for all."

"True story?"

"True story."

Vincent didn't look happy.

"What's wrong, V?"

"Nothin'. Nothin'. I just never expected you to do something like this. It ain't like you."

"Yeah. I know." Francisco shrugged. "You do what you hafta do, right? For a friend, right?"

The wind kicked up, and Vincent shivered.

"Yo, V, it's cold up here. Let me give you my hoodie."

Francisco was wearing a red hoodie with a single large pocket in the center. He slipped off the hoodie and handed it to Vincent.

"Take this."

Underneath Francisco's red hoodie was another hoodie. A black hoodie. Vincent put on the red hoodie.

"The envelope's in the pocket of your hoodie, all right?"

"Huh?" said Vincent.

"Payment. For the groceries. It's in the pocket of the hoodie. Don't take it out. They got security cameras around here on this platform."

Vincent slipped his hands into the center pocket and felt the envelope.

"Oh. I gotcha."

Vincent hugged himself inside the hoodie for warmth.

"Pay Boom back when you get home, all right?"

"Of course! I'm gonna do that right away."

"Vincent, I'm serious. Pay him back. Pay back Boom."

"Yeah. Okay."

But Vincent seemed distracted.

"You listening, V?"

"Uh-huh."

"I got to get back on campus now. I'm not even supposed to be here."

"They got you on a leash, huh?"

"Kinda."

Francisco picked up the grocery bag and made ready to leave. "Let me know when it's all set with Boom."

"Just like that?" said Vincent.

"What do you mean?"

"We talk for two seconds, then you out of here. You act like you don't even know me."

Francisco held up the bag of groceries. "Look what I'm doing for you! I'm risking everything for you! You think I'd do this for a stranger? I heard you was beaten within an inch of your life. I'm giving you your life back!"

"Oh. I see. So I get my life back, and *you* get *your* life back. But they're two different lives, Francisco. Don't you see?"

Francisco dropped the bag. "Be straight up with me, V. Once and for all. What's your problem?"

"There's no problem, bro. That's the point. This whole deal couldn't work out better for you. You get to get rid of me, you get to get rid of your guilt, and then you get to move on with your life."

Francisco looked into his best friend's eyes for a long time. He didn't know whether to hug Vincent or hit him. Whether to feel pity or anger. "So what is it that *you* want?"

"For things to go back to how they were!"

"Why?"

"Because it never got any better for me than the old times. Look at me now! Look what I'm doin', Fran. Working for a drug dealer. Let's be realistic about *my* prospects."

"I'm sorry, Vincent. I'm trying to help."

"Yeah."

There was a long pause. Francisco looked at his watch and picked up the bag. He had to get back to school.

"You know, I been thinking about the old times, too, Vin. But I don't know. . . . I see them differently than you do. It's nice where I am now. I like it here. I maybe like it more than Harlem."

"You got friends here? Friends like *we* used to be friends? Like the Krew?"

"Of course not. Not even close. But that's all a memory to me now. Gone and dead."

The two old friends stood together on the platform, worlds apart. There wasn't much more to say. The winter wind blew. Francisco turned and left; Vincent stayed. A few minutes later, the New York–bound train came into the station.

Spencer was off in dreamland. He couldn't stop imagining how impressed everyone would be when he showed up at the next party *not* with just a little pot, but with cocaine. Enough for everyone. If he felt like his top-dog status at school was slipping because of Francisco's sudden fame, then this should do the trick: He'd be the coke guy. The life of the party. The center of attention.

Anthony was a bundle of nerves, though. He paced the room, wondering if this whole gang thing wasn't such a good idea.

"Shouldn't Francisco be here by now?" said Anthony.

"I don't know."

"But you've done this before, right? I mean, how does it usually work?"

Spencer shrugged. "I'm not sure."

"You're not sure? But you *have* done this before, haven't you?"

"Coke? Not really. I mean, I never said I had."

"But you implied it!"

"I don't think I implied it. You may have *inferred* it, but that's your fault."

"You do realize what happens if this messes up, don't you? I'm screwed at Harvard! I'm screwed at Yale! I'm screwed everywhere!"

"Those places were pipe dreams anyway, Anthony, and you know it."

Anthony's face dropped in searing offense. The door flew open. Francisco came in.

"You're late!" yelled Spencer. "Where the hell were you?"

"I was getting *this*," said Francisco, dropping the bag of groceries on Spencer's bed. He lifted out the box of cereal.

"What is this? Breakfast?"

"Look for the prize inside."

Spencer popped open the box and discovered that the cereal bag had already been opened and then closed again with tape. He ripped the tape and reached inside. Rainbow-colored flakes exploded onto the floor as he mashed his hand around inside the box. Then he stopped—like he'd gotten shocked. A baggie full of white powder emerged, gripped between his thumb and forefinger. He held it up, looking at it with awe.

"There's fourteen more in there," said Francisco.

Spencer was frozen. He'd never seen cocaine before. He squeezed the baggie, feeling the soft granules.

"If you want to try it, to check it out, don't do it around me," said Francisco. "I never touch that stuff."

Spencer took out more little bags, almost mesmerized. They

piled on his bed like a mound of tiny snowballs. His lips began quivering. He felt a freak-out building in his gut.

"Where do we stash it all?" he asked.

"You don't know where?" screamed Anthony. "What was your plan?"

"I didn't have a plan!" yelled Spencer.

Anthony grabbed Spencer by the collar. "The longer it's here, the more likely it is that I'm going to get into trouble! And I don't want to get burned for this! *You* paid for this dirty cocaine, so you take it and leave!"

Spencer started shoving the baggies back into the box. He closed the lid and pushed it at Francisco.

"Take it back."

"What?" said Francisco.

"Take it back to Harlem! I don't want it anymore."

"I can't. The deal's done."

"Then keep the money. Just take it back!" Spencer shoved the box at him again, but Francisco pushed back. Spencer fell to the floor.

"It's your problem now, Spencer. It's your problem! I never wanted to do this in the first place."

Spencer stood up and launched himself at Francisco, pummeling him with his fists. Francisco caught the boy's punches in his hands like tennis balls, wondering how he'd spent sixteen years living in the inner city and not once touching drugs, only to come up *here* to boarding school and turn into a drug dealer. And how this stupid boy, of all people, had gotten him into it.

Then the door flew open again. It was Grand Central Station in here. The three kids stopped and turned. It was that freshman boy again, the one with the red hair and big glasses. The kid's name was Willie.

"Willie!" yelled Anthony. "What're you doing in here?!"

"I made him our lookout," said Spencer.

"Guys! Guys! Shut up for a second!" said Willie. "Dean Archer is coming *right now*!"

Anthony leapt into action. He grabbed the cereal box, ran to the window, and opened it.

"Anthony! Stop!" yelled Willie.

But it was too late: Anthony had thrown the cereal out the window.

Anthony turned to Willie. "What?! I got rid of it!"

"No—Dean Archer is on his way to the *dorm*, you idiot. He's walking over from *his house*!"

Anthony and the others shoved their heads out the window, just in time to witness their futures unravel before their very eyes. Dean Archer was halfway down the short path between his house and the dorm when he was stopped by the sight of a box of cereal dropping onto the walkway in front of Baker Hall. The box broke on impact, and the cereal spilled all over the grass. Dean Archer huffed, and to the kids' abject horror, walked over to the mess and started picking up the scattered sugar flakes.

Then the dean froze. Mixed into the mess on the grass was an array of peculiar-looking little plastic bags. He picked up one, and his jaw dropped.

The dean looked up. His eyes panned straight up the building and settled on a third-floor window in the dorm, where the heads of four shocked students were looking down at him.

April 22

Francisco had never seen such a beautiful room as Straub Hall,
Seton Grove's "old library." It was filled with polished wood
desks, all dark and creaky, and leather couches. The ceiling had
been painted with clouds to make it look like the sky. The building was rarely used these days—except for occasional ceremo-
nies to entertain donors or to give retiring teachers a fancy
send-off. More commonly, though, it was used for DCs—
Disciplinary Committees as they were called—which were the
formal procedures where teachers met to decide the fates of
students who had broken the rules. The students had to wait
in the old library while the teachers debated their cases in a
separate room downstairs.

Francisco, Spencer, and Anthony sat together on a leather
couch. Willie had already been let go with a slap on the wrist.
He was only a bystander, really. He was given a talking-to, and
went back to the dorm, where he looked out the window and
waited for the shock of the whole situation to wear off. Gangs,

drugs, expulsions. He was only fourteen. The strongest drug he'd ever taken was amoxicillin. How had this happened to him?

To any of them?

"This is all your fault, you know," Spencer said to Anthony.

"My fault? How is any of this my fault?"

"Because you threw the bag out the window."

"There wouldn't have even been a bag if you hadn't bought those drugs."

"You're right. So it's Francisco's fault."

Francisco shook his head. "I think it's all our faults."

Spencer sighed. "How diplomatic of you. Well, that's not going to be my story to the DC. I'm not going down for this. I'm going to deny everything. That's what my dad says you do when you get caught for something. Deny *everything*."

And on that depressing note, the other two kids hung their heads. Anthony began to cry.

Click.

The back room door opened. In walked Dean Archer. He wore a plaid tie, a navy blazer, and a sour expression on his face.

"Gentlemen," he said, in a low, threatening tone like distant thunder. Francisco, Anthony, and Spencer stood up. Even Spencer, for all his cockiness, felt nervous. His shoulders shook a little.

"Gentlemen," the dean began again, probably just to sound terrifically dramatic, "I want you and you"—he pointed at Spencer and Anthony—"to go outside so that I can talk to Francisco-o-o." He drew out Francisco's name like that. "So go on, get out of here."

The two confused boys turned and walked out of the library.

The door closed softly behind them. Once they were gone, the dean leaned against a grand piano and looked over his glasses at Francisco.

"Francisco, I hate to be the one to tell you, but we've decided to expel you. You'll have to have your bags packed and be out of here by six o'clock tonight. I'm sorry, but that's how it is."

"You're sorry?" said Francisco, stunned.

"Yes, I am. But you didn't do yourself any favors. This whole scheme of yours was . . . dangerous and irresponsible, to say the least."

"Scheme of *mine?*"

"That fact is beyond discussion at this point."

"Who said it was my scheme?"

"Listen, we know what happened, okay? There's no use denying it now."

Francisco looked out through the glass doors of the library. Spencer and Anthony were on the sidewalk, lightly shivering in the rain. The boys' navy sport jackets blew around in the wind. The gray rain washing across the green campus looked somehow beautiful.

"We tried contacting your parents," said the dean.

"You did?"

"But no one answered the phone. We also don't have an e-mail address on file for them."

"They don't have e-mail. And they work a lot."

"All the same, we need to get you off campus ASAP."

"So, are they expelled, too?" asked Francisco. "My roomates?"

"Don't think about them. Think about yourself."

So Francisco did. He thought about the street fair——the

morning before Vincent got arrested. Before all this trouble began. And he thought about Reignbow. It had been a long time since he'd thought of her. He remembered kissing her at the street fair.

"I can't go home," Francisco said to Dean Archer. He couldn't imagine facing everyone.

"Well, you have to."

"There's nothing there for me. Nothing!"

Dean Archer stuck out his hand for Francisco to shake it. "Good luck to you."

Francisco felt off balance, and he reached for the hand not as much to shake it as to steady himself. Francisco's other hand came up and found itself at the top button of the dean's collared shirt. He gripped down on it.

"You don't understand. I *can't* go home," said Francisco, now balling a fist against the dean's Adam's apple.

"Listen, calm down," said the dean, struggling to get a full breath.

"You can't expel me!"

"Get your hands off me and *calm down*."

Francisco shoved Dean Archer against the piano. "This is bullshit!"

"You're already in a lot of trouble, boy. Don't make it worse for yourself."

Francisco gave him a big shove, then pulled away and stormed out of the library.

"You're lucky we didn't call the cops on you!" yelled Dean Archer, coughing and clearing his throat. "*That* would have been a different cup of tea for you!"

Francisco stormed out across the campus, leaving a dark trail through the fallen rain that glistened on the grass. He hurried past Anthony and Spencer, heading toward the dorm.

"What happened?" yelled Anthony.

But Francisco ignored him.

"Let him go," said Spencer.

Francisco tore across campus. He wanted to dig his fingers into the grass, rip away the lawns. He wanted to knock down buildings with his shoulders.

He made it to his room, feeling like he was going to die of a heart attack, and that's when the tears came. Months of disappointment, pain, and anger. There was nothing he could do about it but scream into his pillow.

Outside his window, life went on across the quad, just as it would tomorrow without him. Had anything been achieved by his time here? Other than putting up some points on the scoreboard? Other than creating a stir among the gossip hounds? Would Spencer and Anthony even remember him years from now, other than their having roomed with "that ghetto kid"?

Francisco opened the closet and took out his backpack and duffel bag. One by one, he pulled out his dresser drawers and moved clothes and toiletries into the bags. The whole operation took less than eight minutes. He scanned the room to see if he'd left anything behind. Nope. He'd removed all evidence that once upon a time there was a boy from the inner city who lived here, who had gotten accepted to the best high school in the country, who had dreamed big—and failed trying.

"Whatchoo want?"

"I'm looking for Boom."

"What fo'?" said the thug.

"What business is it of yours?" challenged Vincent. "I got a present for him."

"What kind of present?"

"Teddy bear. Now, where is he?"

The two thugs glared at Vincent. They were standing at the rear basement door behind the Witterberg Projects, building 13.

"Wait a second," said one of the thugs. "You owe Boom, right?"

"That's right."

"I recognized you. Well, he's gone. The office downstairs got busted, and Boom ain't here no mo'. He laying low."

"Great. So where am I supposed to find the man?"

"Go here." The thug wrote an address on a piece of paper. It was a street corner about ten blocks away.

"You input that address into your mind, okay?" said the thug.

"Okay."

"You memorized it?"

"Yeah."

"Good." Then the thug tore up the piece of paper and threw the pieces at Vincent. "Be there in one hour. Boom will meet you."

Twisting on the toe of his shoe, Vincent ground a hunk of broken windshield glass into the sidewalk. It crumbled into a hundred tiny gemstones. He picked one up and studied it, wondering if he could make a few bucks selling these as precious stones, then thought better of the idea and tossed it away.

He sighed. Boom was late.

Across the street, there was a car that looked like it had been bombed. The windows were blown out, and instead of seats and upholstery, there were just springs and a blackened steel frame. The roof was caved in. The presence of the wreck seemed like a bad omen to Vincent.

He shook his head, trying to clear his thoughts. That argument with Francisco had stuck with him, darkening his already bleak mood. He'd confessed to being a loser, a waste of a life. It hurt to say those things, but even more, it hurt because it was true. Seeing that river upstate, breathing that clean air . . . it broke his heart. It was nice up there, *real* nice, and it was impossible to imagine how he'd ever get to live that kind of life himself. He wasn't book smart, that's for sure. He had only average athletic ability. Good looks and a winning smile was about all he had going for him, and those things barely got him down the block safely anymore, much less far beyond the city, to some life of luxury and ease.

No, Vincent was stuck in Harlem for good. A lifer. And being homeless, he didn't even have his good looks anymore. There was a time he felt like a king in this 'hood, and now he was sleeping on floors, getting kicked in the face. He'd become the scum he used to see staggering around these streets and laugh at, not so very long ago.

Vincent clenched his jaw in resolve. He couldn't make himself smart. He couldn't make himself talented. . . . But he *could* make himself strong. You can buy that type of strength. For the first time since Francisco left Spanish Harlem, Vincent had to consider the possibility that the Krew was truly dead. That Francisco was gone for good. Vincent was alone now, and to make it alone, he had to be a survivor. He only needed the strength to make it.

With no sign of Boom anywhere, Vincent turned and started walking. Before long, he was running, hard cash in his pocket. He felt free to go wherever he wanted. Damn, he'd never thought of the things he could do with this kind of money. To hell if he was going to give it up to some fool who wanted him dead. Six hundred dollars? He could rent a hotel room for a month, sleep on a real bed, eat McDonald's breakfast, lunch, and dinner. His thoughts soared at the possibilities.

He ran east toward Spanish Harlem, where he'd heard about a guy named Raven. Raven, if the rumors were true, could give Vincent exactly what he needed. Power. A presence on the streets again.

It was easy to miss Raven, though. Dude owned a watch repair shop, but to get there, you had to find this Chinese-Mexican restaurant called Fung Wah Baja, over on 108th. Through the smells of corn tortillas and pork fried rice, a small set of stairs led half a story down below Fung Wah Baja, into Raven's repair shop.

Vincent leapt down the stairs with a full head of steam and stormed into the cramped, musty shop. It smelled like shoe leather and grease inside. A door chime crashed above Vincent's head, announcing his arrival. An old woman standing at Raven's glass counter clutched her purse and whipped around in alarm. "Sorry," said Vincent, closing the door more gently. "Didn't mean to scare you."

Raven, who was touching the gears of the old woman's watch with a wooden pick, looked up calmly. He was a Pakistani fellow with a gray walrus mustache and a large magnifying lens strapped to his head. "Can I help you?" he asked.

Vincent didn't answer. Just stood there. Raven nodded to himself and went back to work. "I'll be with you in a moment, sir," said Raven.

A minute later, he closed the woman's watch, set the correct time, and handed it over.

"How much do I owe you?" the old woman asked.

Raven waved his hand. "Please. It only took a moment. You have yourself a nice day."

She slid the watch onto her wrist, nodded thanks, and headed out. Once she was all the way up the steps, Raven went to the door, twisted the deadbolt, and ran the window blind cords down until the sunlight streaming in was choked to nothing and darkness enveloped the shop. Raven paused to give Vincent another serious look.

"You're too young to be a cop."

"Too hip, too," said Vincent.

Raven slid open a hidden cabinet by the floor and lifted out a tray full of handguns. "Let me know if you have any questions."

Vincent looked down the line of guns. Some were small and compact, and looked like they could fit in the palm of a hand. Others were larger, with clips and solid grips, like the ones he'd seen cops carrying. Vincent didn't know much about guns, but he knew, from an aesthetic perspective, what was cool and which gun would give him what he needed.

"That one," Vincent said, pointing to a long-barreled handgun that reminded him of the gun Clint Eastwood carried in his *Dirty Harry* movies.

"Forty-five Long Colt. You're a man of style, I can tell."

Vincent smiled at the compliment and fixed his hair. "How much?"

"For you, my friend, for a man with style such as yourself, five hundred sixty-five dollars."

"You got yourself a deal."

Vincent handed over the money and picked up the gun. He liked the weight of it, the solidness of the barrel. He posed with the gun in different positions, pointing it around the store.

"How do I look?" asked Vincent.

"You look good."

"Yeah?"

"Yes, sir. You look like a man who is not to be messed with."

Vincent lined up the gun sights and pulled the trigger, sounding a small click in the empty chamber. Vincent grinned. "Damn right. I'm not to be messed with. Let every fool know—Vincent's back in the game."

56

"Oh my God! Francisco, you're home!"

Viviana ran across the living room and enveloped Francisco in her arms. "My baby!"

"Yeah, it's me, Ma. It's me."

Francisco dropped his bags at the door. His tie was loosened around his collar. His face showed pure exhaustion, but still he managed to give her a smile. She squeezed him some more. Ernesto calmly walked over and shook Francisco's hand.

"Welcome home," he said.

"But I don't understand!" squealed Viviana. "What is this? What are you doing home?"

"I . . ." He took a breath.

"Yes?"

"I graduated early, Ma. I just graduated."

"You did?"

"Yeah. 'Cause I did so good on my mid-terms. They let me graduate early."

"That's amazing."

"Yeah, it was just me and a couple other guys."

"Oh, my. When?"

"This morning. There was a little——I guess you could call it a ceremony. In this beautiful old library they got up there."

"But I'm confused. Why didn't you tell us? We would have come up for it!"

"Oh, well, you didn't miss much. It wasn't much of a ceremony. Anyway, I'm home now."

Viviana hugged him one more time with all her might. None of his story made much sense, but she was so happy that she couldn't see through it. Her boy was home; nothing else mattered.

"My Francisco," she said. "A high school graduate!"

"Yeah. Ain't that something?" said Francisco. His smile flickered. It was getting harder to keep it up. He averted his gaze from his dad, who had a suspicious expression on his face. Happy to have Francisco home, yes, but suspicious, too.

Francisco went nearly limp in her arms.

"Are you okay, honey?" she asked. "You seem tired."

"Yeah, I'm a little tired. Long train ride."

"I understand." She pulled away and drank him in with her eyes. "My goodness, you look so grown up! Are you hungry?"

"No, I'm not hungry."

"Would you like something to drink?"

"No."

He unloaded his bags off his shoulders, dropped them to the floor. "I just need to rest."

"You don't want anything? Are you sure?"

"I'm positive."

"I have a whole lot of stuff in the fridge. Things you like."

"Thanks, Ma. But I think I'm gonna be in my room now."

"You will?" She seemed deflated.

"Yeah. Just taking a nap."

"Okay."

"It's good to be home, Ma."

"Listen, I have a great idea." She clapped her hands. "We'll have a party for you, okay?"

"Another party?" he said wearily. "With all the relatives?"

"Only when you're ready. When you're up for it."

"Okay, Ma. That'd be good, I guess."

"Oh, and, Francisco—just one more thing."

"Yeah?"

"Let me see your diploma."

"What?"

She got a huge smile and walked over to the TV, above which hung his middle-school graduation photo. She removed the picture from the wall. Behind it, there was nothing but a nail and a shiny square of paint protected from years of dust. "I want to hang it right here," she said. "So I can always see it."

Francisco felt his mouth go dry. "Uh, see, Ma, they got to mail it to me."

"Oh."

"Yeah. They say they ain't printed them yet."

"Okay. I can wait."

He gave her a smile and disappeared into his room, shutting his door and looking out his window. Eighteen stories below, kids were playing in the Dumpsters, finding beer bottles and crashing them against the building.

Quite a homecoming, indeed.

Francisco lay in bed and gazed up at the ceiling. Same old ceiling; same old cracks. He wondered now if he'd be looking at these cracks for the rest of his life.

Knock knock knock.

"Come in, Ma!" said Francisco, sighing.

The door opened, and Ernesto pushed his head through.

"Francisco, could I come in for a minute?"

"Uh, sure." Francisco sat up. He moved over so his dad could sit down. Ernesto clapped a hand on his son's knee.

"It's nice to have you home, you know. It makes us very happy. It was hard for us while you were gone."

"Well, no one has to feel bad anymore." He grinned gamely.

"But *you* feel bad. I can see it in your eyes."

"Me?"

"What happened up there, Francisco?"

"What d'you mean? I'm finished with that school."

"I know you are." His dad leveled his eyes. "Tell me what happened."

"They . . . they threw me out."

There was a long pause while Ernesto absorbed the news. "Why?"

"I don't really know."

"You don't? I don't believe that."

"It just all got to be too much for me."

"They don't kick people out for getting overwhelmed, Francisco."

Francisco squirmed on the bed and, for such a big kid, appeared to shrink a bit.

"You *really* want to know what I did?"

Ernesto paused. This was a good kid, here. Whatever Francisco did wrong, he'd already paid the price, and Ernesto didn't think he deserved any more embarrassment. "Only what you want to tell me."

"Well, I guess I showed them the worst of me, Pop. That's what I did. Of us. I showed them the worst of all of us. I didn't help anything."

His dad put an arm around Francisco's shoulder.

"Did anyone get hurt?"

"No. Just me. And now you."

"Do you think they'd let you back in?"

Francisco shook his head. "Probably not."

His dad sighed and stood up. He took a basketball trophy off Francisco's desk. "I remember when you won this." He smiled, and then beamed. "If you want to know if I'm proud of you, I am." He took a breath. "I hope you're not afraid of the disappointments in life, Francisco, because these things are going to happen. I just hope this experience doesn't make you afraid. There'll be another path for you, another opportunity."

He put down the trophy.

"Did they have a good squad up there?"

"No. They sucked. I got nothing from the other guys on the court. No support. No help."

"Then it sounds like it's good you're not there anymore. It sounds like they didn't deserve you."

Francisco pushed his hands up to his face, hiding his tears. Ernesto kissed the top of his boy's head and then opened the bedroom door.

"I won't say anything about this to your mother. We'll fig-ure out how to break it to her later."

"Okay," mumbled Francisco.

"Come out later for some dinner. You should eat. You got too skinny."

"Okay. . . . Pop?"

"Uh-huh?"

"Thank you."

Francisco lay back. He felt a strange feeling in his stomach. He realized that for the first time since school began, he had nothing to do. No homework. No tests to get ready for. Noth-ing. He couldn't imagine anything getting him out of bed now. An earthquake couldn't lift him out. He wondered what he would do with himself for the rest of the day, or tomorrow, or even for the rest of his life.

57

June 14

Weeks had gone by with Francisco living, essentially, in his bedroom. He emerged on rare occasions like an injured turtle from its shell, to grab a quick bite or take a shower. With his lights off and window shades drawn, Francisco's room was in constant nighttime, while across the city, it was June and summer was in full swing. The streets were loud with teenagers, busy with girls with hiked-up skirts. But Francisco saw none of it. Depressed, sleeping all the time, the only place he could stand to open his eyes and breathe was in the shower. The warm water massaged his face, and the sound drowned out the rest of the world. He'd gotten used to the quiet up at Seton Grove.

When he turned off the water, Francisco heard his mother crying to Ernesto. "He's so sad! What's wrong with him?"

Francisco also heard his father comforting her. "Shhh. He'll come out of it. He just needs some time to readjust. He'll be okay."

Francisco guessed that his dad hadn't told his mom the

truth yet. He went into his room and got dressed. Then he left the apartment without saying anything to either of them.

Out on the streets, Francisco was a ghost. Nobody stopped to shake his hand or welcome him back; nobody even looked at him. Old folks, kids his age—they all ignored him. His life had changed since Veterans Day weekend when he returned as some kind of hero. Word had gotten around about what he said at the Thing, and rumors swirled that he stole Reignbow's money, abandoned his friends, and sunk Vincent into debt. It didn't matter that the rumors weren't entirely true. The gossip was good, and if gossip sounds juicy enough—as he learned first-hand at Seton Grove—then people will blindly believe it.

Sick of his own home, uncomfortable on his own streets, he headed to Reignbow's building, hoping for some love there. Outside her building, Francisco covered his brow and looked up twenty-four stories to see if he could see her window. The best memories of his life were in that room, his times with Reignbow. It was weird how since leaving school, all he could do was think about the past. Up at Seton Grove, he had wanted to leave his past behind and move on with his life. But now he knew that without his memories, he had nothing.

He took a deep breath and went inside.

In the elevator going up, Francisco knew he only wanted to do one thing. To apologize.

I'm sorry, Reignbow—for everything.

He knocked on the door and called Reignbow's name. After a minute, Lily answered.

"What do you want?" she said, with a bitter tone that caught him off guard. She looked fatter and smaller than he'd remembered. Older.

"Hi, Lily. How are you?"

He bent down for a hug and a kiss on the cheek, but she pulled away. "What do you want?"

"Me? Nothing. I was wondering if Reign's around."

"Well, she's not."

"Do you know when she'll be back? I have something I want to tell her."

Lily sighed. "Reignbow has her own life now, Francisco. And you have yours. I think it's best to keep it that way, don't you?"

Francisco looked pained.

"You saying she's dating someone?"

"I didn't say that. I'm saying she has a *life*. A life of her own."

"So I can't come in?"

"Listen to me, Francisco. My daughter is in pain. I used to care for you. I loved you like my own son. You know that, right?"

"Yeah."

"But you lied to her. You took my money. Then you don't call her or nothing. I mean, who do you think you are?"

"I don't know—"

"You hurt her, Francisco. And when she's in pain, *I'm* in pain."

"I didn't mean to hurt anyone. I just don't know what else to do. I got nowhere else to go right now. I mean"—he looked at his hands for an answer—"I didn't plan on leaving how I did. It was just crazy, the emotions I was feeling."

"You were full of yourself. That's all. Full of your own ego. It looks like you've come down from that now. But I can't let Reignbow be the one to catch you as you fall. I won't let her get dragged into your problems again."

"I understand. . . ."

"You do?"

It killed him. "Yes. You know I love you, Lily. Right? You and your daughter. I'm sorry again."

He turned and walked down the hall, hit the button for the elevator. One elevator was working, the other was not. He waited twelve minutes for the elevator to come. When it did, there was a fresh puddle of piss on the floor. He stepped inside but kept his feet to the edge so his shoes wouldn't get wet, and the elevator dropped for what felt like a hundred miles down.

Back at home he slammed his bedroom door shut and screamed, "No one come in!" He imagined never coming out again. Rejected at school, rejected at home, neither world wanted anything to do with him.

So he wanted nothing to do with the world.

Francisco went over to his trophy collection. Gleaming, golden, proud. He drew his arm back and sent them smashing against the wall. He flipped his desk and sent its piles of magazines, CDs, and mail flying across the floor.

In his parents' bedroom, Viviana startled at the loud sound and looked to Ernesto, who pulled her close. More bangs and yelling. It sounded to them like Francisco was ripping his room apart. And indeed, he was; within minutes, there were clothes scattered all around his floor, books ripped and strewn everywhere. Pieces of broken trophies were halfway buried in the mess.

Exhausted, Francisco staggered back against the wall and

caught his breath. He surveyed the terrible mess he'd made, slapping his hand across his eyes and holding it there until he could force himself to calm down.

He went over to one of his trophies and picked it up. The golden basketball player leaned off its marble base at a harrowing angle.

"Damn."

He turned it upside down. A big screw stuck out; it was loose and spun freely in his fingers.

Somewhere, on his desk, he used to keep a screwdriver. With the contents of his desk now spread out like carpeting, Francisco started lifting piles of junk and dropping them back down. He moped a bit while he searched, feeling like a mournful Godzilla trying to somehow make sense of the destruction he'd wrought, trying to find the bodies he'd flung all around.

Francisco didn't find the screwdriver, but he did find a piece of mail: an envelope, unopened, and addressed to him. Seton Grove was written on the return address. The postmark date was stamped two days ago. His mom or dad must have put it on his desk while he was getting shut out over at Reignbow's. The Latin words *ad astra per aspera* showed through the white envelope. *From the stars, into difficulty*, thought Francisco, twisting the translation of the motto.

He couldn't imagine what was in the letter. What else could they do to him? What else could they say? He considered throwing it straight into the trash, but instead, he stuck his finger into the crease and pulled. The envelope came apart in his hands as if there were a small bomb inside. Amid all the pieces, he found a letter.

Dear Mr. Ortiz, we want to extend our regrets for the circumstances of Francisco's expulsion. In an effort to rectify all parties' possible complaints, we are reimbursing you for the unused remainder of Francisco's tuition. . . .

Francisco stopped reading. Reimbursing? He flipped the letter over and found a check made out to Mr. Ernesto Francisco Ortiz.

Even more incredible, though, was the amount: $1,650.38.

Francisco stared at the check. *It did not rightfully belong to him*, that much he knew. But there it was, in his hands, and it was even more strange to see his own name on it. He and his dad shared the same name, Ernesto Francisco Ortiz—but Francisco went by his middle name, and his dad went by his first.

The name was certainly familiar in the family, passed down for generations, but the more Francisco read the letter, the stranger his name sounded, and the less familiar it felt, as if he wasn't Francisco Ortiz at all. Whoever he was—a kid from the ghetto or a prep school kid, a no-good drug dealer or a dedicated student with a good future—whoever *Francisco Ortiz* really was, he'd never been someone who had $1,650.38 lying around.

Francisco needed to think. Slipping the check into his pocket, he went out to Hope Park. Sitting by himself on a bench, he started considering the possibilities. One thought was to return the check to the school, out of principle. But he'd felt so bruised by the past months' experiences that he wasn't sure he had the luxury to even *have* principles.

Another thought was to give it to his parents. They could certainly use the money. But to do so would raise all kinds of questions and ultimately lead to him having to confess to his mom what really happened. It would break her heart. Shatter it.

Paralyzed with indecision, he folded the check and slipped it back into his pocket.

Right on time, as it turned out. Two guys walked into the park. One was big and ugly. He had stupid, angry eyes carved deeply into his head. The other guy was small and had a sad, twitchy little face. He wore a T-shirt with a stop sign on it and the words STOP SNITCHING.

Francisco gave the two guys a cautious nod. No one ever came in here. They walked toward Francisco, whispering to each other and kind of nodding around to the flowers and sculptures of the park.

Then they sat down on Francisco's bench. One on either side of him. Too close for comfort.

"Do I know you?" said Francisco, not sure who to talk to.

"I'm a friend of a friend," said the short guy, the talker. The only one who talked.

"What friend?"

"Vincent. You a friend of Vincent, right?"

"Yeah. Why?"

" 'Cause I'm looking for Vincent, and I thought maybe you could help us out."

Francisco cocked his head. "You're that dude Boom, aren't you?"

"That I am."

"Well, Vin paid you back. So what d'you want with me?"

Boom laughed. "Actually, bro, you're mistaken. He never paid me back."

Francisco gauged Boom's eyes, searching to see evidence of lying. The eyes disturbed Francisco. Watery and murky like two pools of open sewage. "You're lying," said Francisco.

"Try me, fool."

"I got him the money myself. I know for a fact he paid you."

"Nigga, you about to call me a liar again?"

"No. But he promised me."

"He promised me, too. Clearly his word means nothing. I hope your word is a lot better than his."

"What d'you mean?"

"I need your help, nigga. I need you to go to your buddy Vincent and make sure that he pays me."

"Me? C'mon. I did my part. More than my part. And anyway, you put him in the hospital! Almost killed him! Why should I help you?"

"Because if you don't, I'ma send *you* to the hospital. Understand me? If I can't collect from Vincent, then I'ma collect from you." He pressed his finger into Francisco's cheek.

Francisco swatted him away. "That's not fair, man. You have *no idea* what I went through to make sure he had the money."

"Fair? Come on. I heard you're a big-shot prep-school kid. You got your whole life laid out ahead of you. You're the one who's got a future. So what do you care about what's fair in these here streets?"

60

June 19

Jason finally made it to the courts. The temperature spiked into the nineties for the first time all year, and his mom more or less shoved him out of the house. "I swear, you watched TV for about six straight months. That's enough," she said. "Go out and breathe some air, boy."

He headed down the street by himself, his basketball—slightly deflated from lack of use—tucked under his arm. He'd graduated from high school the week before. Like Reignbow, Boonsie, and Dink, and every other kid in New York City. But he'd graduated alone at his and Vincent's school in Harlem. Vincent hadn't been seen at school for the whole semester, so Jason stood alone, his blue gown flowing out over his big belly like he was hiding another person underneath. A frown was shoved in between his large cheeks. None of it was fun.

And it still wasn't fun, out on the basketball courts alone, playing ball with nobody. He threw up a few shots, then sat down against a flagpole to catch his breath.

That's where Francisco found him. Francisco came over and sat down. It was the first conversation Francisco had had with another kid, even with the Krew, since he'd returned home. Jason, it seemed, was the only kid who would talk to him.

" 'Sup?"

" 'Sup," said Jason, unhappy to see him.

"What's good with you?"

"Nuthin'."

"Whatchoo been doing?" asked Francisco.

"Me?"

"Yeah."

"What's it look like I'm doing? Shit. Damn you blind."

"Whoa, whoa. Why you goin' off like that?"

Jason sighed and shook his head. "What are you doin' back?"

"I . . ." Francisco started to say, but realized he didn't have it in him to lie anymore. "I got kicked out."

Jason laughed. "You serious?"

"Yeah."

"After all that shit, huh?"

"Uh-huh."

"You screwed."

"I know."

"But I guess we all are. Do you know how bad it is to even be seen with you, F?"

"Me?"

"Yeah!"

"Why me?"

"Everyone knows what you did. What you put Vincent through."

Francisco yelled, "Oh, and *I'm* the one responsible for him acting crazy?"

"No, but when I called you for help, I never expected *this* was gonna be your plan for helping him out. I wouldn't have asked you if I thought you were gonna pull off a drug deal. We expected you to be the smart one, you know."

Francisco nodded. "I know. I know. . . ."

"You *recruited* Vincent, turned him into a drug dealer, F. You acted like a white dude up there exploiting a black dude just to make money. Now he lost in life. He don't have nothing. Not even a high school diploma like the rest of us. Well, I guess it's sort of funny that you don't have one either."

Francisco shook his head. The whole thing sounded even crazier hearing it altogether like this.

"I was just trying to help, Jason. And I mean, it almost worked. Vincent had the money. I helped him get the money. What happened?"

"He screwed it up. He's always a screwup."

"I did everything I could for that kid. But he blew it."

"And you blew it, too, F." Jason turned his hulking body away. He tried to look mad, but Jason couldn't be mad much longer than he could hold his breath, and his anger broke into sadness. Shook his head again. There was nothing but defeat coming from this sad kid.

"I know that, Jase. But it goes deep between me and Vin. Yo, like for real, Jase, this is how I feel: When I left, everybody kept telling me, 'Oh, up there, when you go to school, you're going to change.' But it's like I come back here, and I'm not the one that changed. Everybody else has changed. This place has changed."

"I don't know about that," said Jason. He scanned the graffiti-covered buildings, the garbage bags piled head-high on the streets. "It looks like the same old shit to me."

"But you have to see it from my eyes. You don't know what it's been like up there with nobody you know, kids you've never been with, making stereotypes and assumptions about who you are. And then I come home, and there's nothing here for me either. I just get all this heat. Haters. Gossip. It ain't fair, man. It's not fair."

"Tell me about it."

"I lost my only opportunity, Jase, my only shot. To see the world." Francisco's words sounded stupid even to himself. Corny. Who'd he think he was talking to? Oprah? He wondered if Vincent had been right all along; if his grand ambitions weren't just clichés. Something stupid he'd seen on TV too many times.

A truck horn blared. Across the street, a mother was yelling at her baby. Francisco held back tears. "I can't even see Reignbow nomore. And now I got this dude Boom up *my* ass."

"Boom?"

"Uh-huh."

"Man, this shit ain't never gonna end. It only gonna get worse."

"No, I'm gonna end it, Jason. I'm gonna fix things right this time. Get the Krew back the way it used to be. But I got to find Vincent. You know where he's gone?"

Jason said nothing.

"Yo, I'm pleading with you an' shit, Jason. This is for real. It's life or death."

"The Krew ain't been a crew for a while, you know? We all split up. Doing our own things or doing nothing at all. It ain't like it used to be."

"I know that. And I guess that's my fault, too. I got a lot of fixing to do, Jason. But I need your help." Francisco looked straight into his eyes. "Tell me where Vincent is."

"His moms can't even find him. She back from Florida, you know? And now she looking for him, too. She says she's sober, sober for good now, and wants her boy back. Everyone's worried, but even she don't know where he is. No one does."

"But you do."

"Vincent made me promise not to say."

"*Tell me.*"

Jason dropped the slightly deflated ball on the ground and stomped it with his foot, popping it. "Everything's gone to hell anyway. I'm tired of carrying around that boy's problems." He leveled his gaze at Francisco. "Ai'ight, I'll tell. But be prepared, Fran. This shit ain't pretty."

61

Sunlight streamed into an abandoned fifth-floor loft in upper Harlem. Old food wrappers and newspapers and used condoms cluttered the floor. Illuminated by the light, particles of dust drifted like snow, accumulating on the walls into a fine fur. There was a fireplace filled with black bags of trash and rat traps in the corners. Classic New York City squatter's apartment.

Scrrreech!

There wasn't so much a door in the room (at least, not a door attached to a doorway) as there was a metal hatch, like a submarine hatch, built into the brick of the back wall. A hand was punching the rusty hatch open—*screech screech screech*—and when the opening was wide enough, Francisco crawled through. He stood up and looked around: He'd never been in a squat before.

It stank.

Right off, Francisco recognized some of Vincent's clothes wadded up in one corner. Jason was right—Vincent had been living here at one point. The question was, was he living here now? In another corner, Francisco saw a dead bird. It seemed so peculiar to see it just sitting there inside this shuttered room. It had a beautiful, flecked coat, and Francisco wondered for a moment if it was even real. Strangely, there was also rubble all over the floor. Francisco used a small rock to flip the bird over. Underneath, the bird was rotted and full of black gristle.

He picked up things as he went, examining them: half-emptied beer bottles with cigarette butts soaking inside, smoked joints, random silverware. There was no sign that Vincent had been here recently, but Francisco had no choice other than to have a seat, get comfortable, and wait.

An hour later, the window slammed open, and Vincent crawled in from the fire escape. When he saw Francisco, Vincent immediately started laughing.

"Ho-ho! Yo, Francisco, my dude! You came to visit!"

Francisco sat up on the mat, brushing off clumps of dust. "Sort of."

"I like to see you just chillin' here. Whatchoo think of my place? It's a good crib, right?" Vincent hugged Francisco.

"It's a shit hole."

"It's my crib, baby. Welcome home."

Francisco pointed to the corner of the room. "Did you know there's a dead bird in your crib?"

"Yeah . . . I know. I don't know how that little dude got there."

"But that thing's *dead*."

"It's fine."

"It's not fine. It's not natural."

"He resting in peace. I'm leaving the little guy alone. He ain't bothering me, damn. . . . So what's good with you?"

Francisco cocked his head to the side. "Why are you acting so damn happy?"

" 'Cause I *am* happy. Oh, I know it's quiet up here. But I like the peace and quiet."

"You like the quiet, huh?"

"True story. Reminds me of upstate." Vincent plopped down on the mattress, and dust shot up, enveloping him. "So, what's good, Francisco?"

Francisco couldn't stop looking around the place. He pointed over at the floor. "Also, you have a door in the, uh, middle of your floor."

"Yeah, see, there's somethin' wrong with the floor. It's sort of *missing* in that particular spot. So I put that door down to make it look like a warning sign. So niggas know not to step on that spot. You step on that spot, and you be *gone*. But that's the only real problem with this place. This place is good. *I'm* good."

"You are? Are you hallucinating, or are you in a dreamworld?"

"Come on, sit down. Make yourself comfortable."

Francisco remained on his feet. "Yo, I heard from a friend of yours."

"You did? I hope she was sexy."

"He wasn't. Ugliest motherfucker I seen in a while. Bulldog ugly. Called himself Boom."

"Boom? What he want with you?"

"He wanted me to know that you ain't paid him his money yet."

Vincent waved his hands in the air. "And now you all worried, huh? But don't worry about that. Fact is, I'm hustling, and I'm grindin' right now. It might take me some time, but I'm gonna pay that dude back."

"Don't worry about it?"

"No. I'm crashin' right here and laying low till I get the money."

"But Vincent, you *already* had the money. What happened to the money I got you?"

"Oh, yo, it all went wrong. If you can believe it, I got mugged."

"Mugged?"

"Yeah. Some dude held me up with a knife. Took my six hundred large."

"You serious?"

"Yeah! Yo, it's a rough neighborhood. But I don't need to tell you that. . . . Or maybe I do, with you gone so long and everything. You probably forgot what it's like down here."

Francisco shut his eyes. The tremendous disappointments of life barely hurt him anymore. "V, yo, I got kicked out of school for that money. Some random mugger *really* took it?"

"For real. I know, man. It ain't fair. I know."

"Fair? I was kicked out of school! And now Boom's threatening *me*."

"I *got* this situation, ai'ight?"

"No, you don't!"

Francisco felt like he was going to freak out, break down, and jump out the window. It took all of his strength just to stay calm. "Vincent, what we gotta do is get you and me out of town for a bit. Maybe Jersey, or farther than that. Wait for this whole thing to pass—"

"No. Never. I ain't goin' nowhere. I definitely ain't goin' out of town. I'll be chilling in Harlem till the day I die. Don't you get it? Harlem my home sweet home." He took a deep breath. "If anything, I'ma kick *that* dude Boom out."

"Yeah, right. You seen the dudes he travels with? Never gonna happen."

"Oh, I got a few tricks up my sleeve, too, yo." Vincent smiled in a coy way that Francisco didn't get, but found disturbing.

"Whatever," said Francisco. "If you won't leave, then we should go talk to Boom. Try to reason with him. Maybe he heard something about who mugged you. Maybe we can all work something out."

"No way. I don't want to give Boom the upper hand."

Francisco threw his arms above his head, utterly frustrated. "All right, tough man. All right. Then it looks like you got everything taken care of. Guess you don't need my help, after all."

"Whatchoo mean?"

"I'll catch ya later." Francisco turned around. "How do I get out of here? Window or hatch? Or the door in the floor?"

"Yo, you leavin'?"

"I guess."

Vincent jumped up and grabbed him. "Wait up. You quittin' me?"

"Nothin' else I can do. Nothin' else I wanna do."

"See? I knew it. I knew it all along."

"What?"

"We ain't friends nomore. You went up to that school and

started thinking you were better than me. Better than all of us. You never would have ditched me before you went off."

Francisco started yelling at him. "We always gonna be friends, Vincent! You should know that by now! But you been so scared and testing our friendship that you didn't even realize you were breaking it. I can only take so much!"

Vincent gripped his shirt tighter, desperate. "You can't leave, Fran. You promised me. You *promised*."

"What did I promise?"

"That you'd always be there for me! No matter what. Those were *your* words. 'No matter what.'"

"When the hell did I ever say that?" Francisco roared.

"When we was five! Don't you remember nothing?" Vincent's eyes flushed red and wet. He pressed his palms to his eyes and squeezed out some tears. "Fuck, man, I'm crying. Look at what a mess I am." He blotted his face with the bottom of his shirt. "I remember that shit exactly. My mom was back in detox, and I was living with your family. Sleepin' in your room. Your mom flicked the lights out for bedtime, but I was feeling scared of the dark. I was trembling in my sleeping bag, not knowing if I was gonna have a mom again, much as I hated her. So when Viviana left the room, you turned that light back on. You spoke up and promised me. 'I always gonna help you, Vincent. No matter what. Don't worry 'bout nothing.'" Vincent took a breath and stopped crying. "But now you taking that shit back, huh?"

"Yo. . . ."

"True story. You remember?"

Francisco nodded. "I do," he muttered.

"Good. See, I ain't all that crazy."

Francisco steeled himself. "Ai'ight. I'll help you, dude. But on one condition: You do everything I say. And I mean *exactly*."

"I can do that."

"I'm Steinbrenner now, and you're—"

"Reggie Jackson!" Vincent clapped his hands together.

"Please. You ain't no Reggie Jackson."

"You know I am, Fran."

"Fine. Reggie. I don't care. But it means you listen to me."

"Anything."

"Now, first thing we need to do is go see this dude Boom."

"Okay, I'll meet him, but you wrong in wanting to explain anything to him. He don't work that way. What I vote is, we go and hustle these niggas out."

"What? No."

"We ain't got no more money. What else can we do?"

"Yo, believe me, we gonna pay these dudes back. We gonna give them their money."

"How you gonna pay these dudes back? With what money?"

"I got a check from my school. Okay? They made a mistake with my tuition and sent my folks a check. It's their check, but I think I can cash it."

"They *pay* you for getting kicked out? Shit—"

"No, dumbass. They're just reimbursing me for the tuition I didn't use, 'cause I ain't in school nomore. I'm not eating their food and taking up space in their dorm and shit. My tuition was all paid for by my scholarship, but someone at the school must have messed up and sent me a check anyway."

Vincent's eyes lit up. "You get a lot?"

"Enough to help your ass. And enough to pay back Reignbow."

"That's the craziest thing I ever heard. Free money."

"Yeah, well, I guess they got stupid people everywhere. Even at the smartest schools."

Vincent laughed, then a seriousness fell over him. "It's nice talking to you again, Fran. Talk for real like this. I missed it. We ain't laughed in a while."

"Yeah. It's nice for me, too."

Vincent sighed. "All right. So we pay the dude."

"Exactly. We movin' on from these problems. Start new lives for ourselves. Be free and clear."

Vincent rubbed his face. "So you home for good now, huh?"

"Yeah."

"I'm sorry to hear it." Vincent paused. "I mean it," he said slowly.

"Thanks."

"Just one more thing. When we go see Boom, we got to protect ourselves."

"Hang on. No guns, Vin."

"Who's talking guns? I'm just saying we need more dudes with us."

"Like who?"

"Like our boy, Jase. He'll come. And he a big, big boy. We gonna want that. Not that anything's gonna go wrong, but we gonna want that bigness with us."

Francisco shrugged. "All right. I mean, nothing's going to happen anyway."

"Exactly. Ain't nuthin' gonna happen."

June 28

Ernesto Francisco Ortiz.

Ernesto Francisco Ortiz.

The two names matched perfectly—the one on Francisco's driver's license and the one on the check. Francisco signed his name to a form agreeing to pay Check Cashing 1634 Inc. a $247.56 cut of the check—15 percent—and then waited as the teller counted out his payment in cash.

Francisco looked around the joint. No one else was in here. Concrete floor with a drain in the center. Nothing on the white walls. A few blinking neon signs in the window. The bulletproof glass separating him from the teller was so thick that everything behind it looked warped and greenish.

As the teller continued counting, Francisco thought about Vincent and the promise he'd made to him over a decade ago. He thought about how, when he first saw Vincent, he believed the boy was a ghost. He'd always kinda been a ghost ever since. Vincent was born with doom inside of him.

"You got a bag for me?" asked Francisco.

The teller stuffed the cash in a brown paper bag and pushed it under the window into Francisco's hands.

"Keep away from Foxwoods with this, got it?" said the teller. Francisco glared at her, and then walked out.

Ninety minutes later, he, Vincent, and Jason were heading north on the West Side of Manhattan. They climbed the steep hills and thick forests of Fort Tryon Park. There was no park in the city quite like Fort Tryon, with its towering protrusions of rocky cliffs jutting over hidden paths that circled higher and higher above the city. Old stone military walls lined the tops of the park's peaks.

Francisco, Vincent, and Jason climbed the twisting dirt paths. Vincent led. Jason bumped along behind, grasping at low-hanging branches and pulling his big body forward, losing energy with every step.

As they neared the top of the park, Francisco stopped and waited for Jason to catch up. Francisco looked back at the route they'd hiked, out over the treetops. The city sprawled out far beneath them. In the distance, projects rose up like dark towers toward the setting sun. The sounds of the city played quietly from this distance, like a recording from a century ago.

"Yo, I never realized how beautiful the city is," Francisco said. "It really is."

Vincent gave a careless glance over his shoulder and shrugged. "So what?" he said. "It's just a bunch of buildings." Vincent went on walking. He kept having to pull his jeans up around his waist. The pants were heavy, weighed down by the .45 Long Colt he'd strung up across the groin, hanging secretly inside his pants.

"What's wrong with you?" Francisco asked, watching Vincent hitch his belt up.

"Nothin'."

The threesome walked for another half hour, as the night-time darkness crowded in around them like narrowing canyons, until they reached a small, secluded clearing at the top of the park. In the center of the clearing, lit from the spotlight of the moon, were Boom and RJ sitting on a large boulder.

"Yo! Yo! You niggas got our money, right?" yelled Boom, standing up on the boulder. "Come over here and show me what you got, but do it slow. Pretend you slow dancing, niggas."

"Ai'ight. Just chill," said Francisco. The three boys had to look up at Boom.

Boom pointed down at a weary-looking Jason. "Who invited your fat ass?"

"Fuck your mutha," blurted Jason.

"What'd you say?" yelled RJ, jumping to his feet.

"Chill, chill, everyone," said Boom. "I just want to know one thing and one thing only: You got my money?"

"Nope," said Vincent. "We gonna hustle you motherfuckers."

"So you must be prepared to die then, huh, V-murder?"

"Yeah, and bring you down with me the next time you insult my boy Jason again."

Francisco jumped in the middle and waved his arms like a ref in a boxing match. "Hold on, hold on! I got the money, man. But all this arguing gotta stop—"

"Ain't nothing gonna stop. I'm gonna shoot it up," said Boom.

"Seriously," continued Francisco. "All this beefin' gotta stop."

RJ pointed at Vincent and said, "I'm gonna git you. Remember what I did to your face last time?"

Vincent pursed his lips and made a kissing sound at RJ.

"Oh, you tough now? You tough?"

Vincent glared at him, challenging. "You about to see how tough."

Francisco pulled Vincent back. "Shut up, V," he whispered. "Chill."

"All right, enough!" Boom said. "I need to see this money before anything."

"It's right here." Francisco pulled the brown sandwich bag out of his pocket and handed it to Boom. Boom opened it and grinned, flipping through the bills.

"Make sure you count that shit double. I don't trust no spics around no money," said RJ.

Francisco stared at RJ, clenched his jaw, then looked at the ground. Boom surveyed the boys. " 'Bout damn time. So what took ya niggas so long?"

Francisco shrugged. "It doesn't matter. You got your money, right?"

"Damn right."

Francisco clapped his hands and pushed them out, making the baseball sign for "safe." "Then it's a wrap. We're done."

Silence befell the five noisy young men. Vincent gazed at the trees stretching above them, smelled the forest air. Was it really done? Completely? Beside him, Francisco looked soul-weary. "We're done," Francisco said again. The toll on him was clear. Looked like he'd run a marathon and found no one at the end cheering him on, or waiting for him. He'd lost everything for this quiet moment in the trees and had nothing left for all he'd given.

Vincent hurt to see it. The recognition of what he'd done came clear. He'd wiped out his best friend. Left him supplicating to these fools on the boulder. He and Francisco were famous in these streets once, but now they were just fools to fools. Worthless.

Vincent reached into his pants and, with one finger, flicked a string, like untying a shoe. Francisco heard the thump on the ground, looked down, and saw the barrel of a .45 sticking out of the bottom of Vincent's baggy pant leg.

"V, no," shouted Francisco, the whole world slowing down.

Vincent reached down and picked it up, pointing the gun at RJ and Boom. "We ain't done, fools."

"Vincent," said Francisco again, grabbing at Vincent's hand. "Drop it."

RJ reached back and pulled out his own gun. Jason was already turning on his heel and running.

"We ain't done by a long shot," said Vincent, holding his ground. "We hustling *you* now."

"Go to hell!" screamed Boom.

Francisco punched at Vincent's gun just as Vincent pulled the trigger. The gun fired wide, missing RJ and Boom. "Run!" yelled Francisco. "Run!"

Vincent's gun spun off into some brush. RJ fired, but missed, too. Vincent and Francisco bolted down a rocky, winding path.

Francisco turned to his right, up into the woods. Jason was ahead. It was amazing that that boy with all that girth was faster than him, but however he did it, Jason was throwing his hulking mass along the path like a hovercraft, disappearing into the trees.

Francisco turned and saw Vincent going in an opposite direction, his long, lean body moving fast as blazes. There was an old military guardhouse on the other side of the hill. Vincent was heading for it.

It was late at night now. The woods had tall hills and sudden valleys, and it was disorienting trying to figure out which way led out of the park and to the street versus the paths that headed deeper into the woods.

Amid the confusion, Francisco heard his name being called. It sounded like Vincent's voice, but he couldn't be sure. He ran toward the voice. Then there was a pop from a gun. Francisco stopped. He saw a dark flash behind a tree, then saw a spark from the muzzle—a second flash. It was too dark to see if the gunman was shooting at Francisco or in another direction.

He bolted again.

Two more shots. Then a cry. A cry from his own lungs? Impossible to tell, actually. The shots came faster. Francisco saw a glowing light, perhaps a streetlight, several hundred feet away, through thick clumps of trees and leaves. He ran for the light. He ran faster than he'd ever thought he could run. He would not stop for anything—he would run until he was dead, or until he was found, and as silhouettes darted distantly across the hills around him and above him, and guns flashed and blazed, Francisco thought it was equal odds whether he would die tonight, or live.

PART THREE

NINETY-SECOND POLICE PRECINCT

"Do you know if he felt any pain?"

"Who?"

Reignbow doesn't quite know how to phrase it. In reality, it's not that hard a thing to say. But to utter it—*his name*—would make his killing too real, and she's still having a hard time believing that any of this is real: that she is actually sitting in a police station, being questioned by a cop.

"When he died, I mean."

Molly Keating, detective rank, badge number 3286, softens her eyes toward Reignbow. "I haven't seen the coroner's report, but from what I saw of the body myself, the bullets were mercifully accurate. I think he passed before he really knew what got him."

The realization hits Reignbow: For the first time in her life, she knows someone who is dead. Well, she doesn't know him anymore, because he is no more. And it is that dreary thought that makes her want to cry her eyes out, scream, and hope she wakes up from this awful nightmare.

"I just can't help but feel that it's all my fault," says Reignbow.

"Back to that again. I still don't understand."

"Because I gave him the money. If I hadn't, then none of this would have happened."

"But you couldn't have known where it all would lead. You can't predict the future. How is this your fault?"

"I trusted Francisco. And that was my mistake."

"You loved him. Of course you trusted him. You can't be blamed for that."

"I should have known better," says Reignbow. "I used to think it was just people outside of my neighborhood that you couldn't trust. 'Cause they don't know you, and you don't know them. But I see now that even *inside* the 'hood, inside the Krew, you still can't trust anyone."

"I disagree."

Reignbow shrugs. "That's because you don't know anything about me. You don't know anything about my people or my 'hood."

"Maybe not—but in a way, it's the same everywhere. People need people, Ms. Rivera. You need me to find the killers, and I need your help in order to find them. You don't know me, but you can still trust that I'm going to find the people who killed your friend."

Reignbow goes silent.

"Listen," the detective says. "I want to help. The killers, that busted traffic light—all of it. El Barrio, it's good here. No, it's not my home, you're right, but I can still love coming to work. I can still admire this place. And this place deserves to be fixed up."

"Nothing gets fixed. Yo, in this 'hood, people get away with murder all the time. Cops don't care when folks kill each other in the ghetto. Hell, you all probably see it as a good thing: One less derelict to deal with, right? You won't find them."

"I promise, we're not going to let you down."

"Yeah, right."

"*Yeah, right?*"

"Yeah. Right."

"You know, I've never done this before, Ms. Rivera, and my lieutenant would have my head if he knew about this. But I think you need a good lesson here." Detective Keating pushes her right hand across the table. "Let's bet on it."

"Bet?"

"Yeah."

"On what?" says Reignbow.

"Bet that we're going to find them. The killers."

"You're crazy."

"Yes, this is a little crazy," says Detective Keating. "But it's simple: If we don't find them, then you win the bet."

"What do I get?"

"You get to leave here, free and clear. Go on home to your own water and snacks that I *didn't* poison, and your own assumptions about the world—which you're free to have—but which, in my opinion, close you off from the rest of the world."

Reignbow shrugs. "Ai'ight. Then what happens if *you* win?"

"If we catch the killers, and I win, then you have to promise me something."

"What?"

"That you're going to trust someone again."

"Please. That's stupid."

Keating steadies her hand across the table. "Fine, it's stupid. But if you're so sure, how can you turn down a chance to prove a cop wrong? You'd have bragging rights with your friends."

Reignbow's eyes brighten. "Okay, who do I hafta trust?"

"It doesn't matter. That's the point. In fact, when we do catch the killers, I want you to trust the first person you see. Whoever it is—I want you to open up your heart, and trust them. People will surprise you."

Reignbow lets out a big laugh. "You're the craziest white person I ever met. But ai'ight, it's a deal."

"Shake on it?"

Reignbow grabs her hand. "Deal." They shake hands across the cold aluminum table.

Just then, a knock comes at the door. It opens slightly, and the face of an alarmed young police officer peeks through.

"Detective Keating, we need you out here."

"What's going on?"

"Please. As soon as you can!"

Keating gives Reignbow a quick look, then rushes out the door.

Reignbow follows Detective Keating out of the interrogation room and into the main lobby, where Dinky and Boonsie are sitting on a bench together. The girls look dazed, having faced hours of questioning, and their eyes are thick with the need for sleep. A few handcuffed drunks sleep next to them on the bench. It's after three in the morning.

Reignbow trades little hugs with her girlfriends.

"You guys all right?" says Reignbow.

Yeah . . . yeah, they mumble. But they don't seem all right. Reignbow sits down next to them.

"What's going on out here?"

"I heard they caught the killers," says Dinky.

"What!"

"Yeah. . . ."

Another door to an interrogation room opens, and Jason walks out. He looks like he's been crying, but he hides it as he comes over.

"That cop I was talking to says we can go," says Jason, keeping his head down and his face sort of covered. "Don't need us nomore."

"Do we hafta come back?" asks Boonsie.

"No. But they'll call us if they need anything." He pauses and rubs his eyes. Several detectives and cops rush past them, talking quickly. It's becoming a zoo inside the station.

"I want to go home, but I also kinda don't want to," says Jason. " 'Cause it's like I never gonna see him in the 'hood nomore."

The three girls nod at the sentiment.

"I'm gonna miss him," says Dinky, breaking down.

Reignbow opens her mouth to say something. If anyone should speak up, it's her—she should eulogize the moment. But nothing comes out of her mouth. She's too tired to feel much of anything.

Suddenly, there's a commotion at the front doors of the police station. A crowd of local TV news crews—NY1, ABC, CBS—shining lights and jabbing microphones into the faces of four cops trying to enter the building.

"Check it out," says Reignbow.

The four cops push through the crowd of journalists, dragging Boom and RJ by their arms, their wrists locked in handcuffs. They look dazed, with twigs snaggled in their hair and scratches along their faces. They're staggering or perhaps limping. Camera lights sting their eyes, and they drop their faces to hide. Microphones attack like blunt weapons.

"Oh my God," says Dinky. "That's them. That's *them*."

Reignbow looks across the police station and, with her eyes, finds a proud-looking Detective Keating. Keating locks eyes with Reignbow and gives a sober smile. *I win*, she mouths.

Then Keating points back to the entrance of the police station, past the two killers. Reignbow follows her gaze and finds Francisco walking in through the front door. Francisco, accompanied by several detectives.

Reignbow's heart races.

"Reign?" says Dinky, noticing her friend's intense gaze. "Are you okay?"

Reignbow nods, but she can't quite manage to find her breath.

"Well, I just got to get some sleep," says Boonsie. "I don't feel okay. I'm wrecked." She stands up. Everyone mutters agreement and starts to leave. Except for Reignbow.

"You coming?" asks Dinky.

"I wanna talk to F."

"Okay. Love you lots. Always will."

The girls hug. Jason stands off to the side, watching awkwardly. He gives a little wave and disappears into the streets. Boonsie and Dink head off in the opposite direction.

Reignbow is left alone on the bench, watching from a distance as Francisco talks to several detectives. He has yet to see her.

Then Reignbow notices a lone woman walking into the police station. She wears ragged clothes and a startled, sad expression. It's been years, but Reignbow still recognizes her as Vincent's mom. She looks old now, older than she should look. The years have been bad to her. But, at least, she looks sober.

Reignbow considers going over and offering condolences. But the mother's grief appears staggering, and Reignbow has no idea what she'd say anyway.

The next moment, Reignbow feels a presence behind her. She turns.

"Hey, Reign." It's Francisco.

"Hey," she says, standing up nervously. "Where've you been all night?"

"Nowhere." He shrugs. "Driving around with the cops and looking for those guys. The cops needed me to ID them. We found them hiding in the park. Anyway, it's over now."

"You look tired."

"Yeah."

They stand together in total, awful, uncomfortable silence.

"Anyway," she says, "I should get going. My mom is probably waiting up for me."

"Yeah," says Francisco. "I should go, too." His eyes look deep into her eyes, "Take care, Reign. Take care."

Just like that, he leaves. She watches him walk out of the police station, and takes a moment to look around this place—the misery of the criminals, the intimidating cops, the harsh echoes. This horrible place in the heart of her 'hood. Reignbow puts her head up high, and walks out into the late-night streets of Spanish Harlem.

July 2

No weapon that is formed against thee shall prosper.
—Isaiah 54:17

The windows of the storefront church on 133rd Street are covered with handwritten signs of Bible quotes. In the street, a rusted-out twenty-year-old Cadillac hearse is parked against the curb. The meter has run out, and a tiny red flag sits up in the glass encasement endlessly hailing a meter maid. A small blue placard that reads FUNERAL sits crookedly on the dashboard of the hearse, the only defense against a ticket.

Inside the funeral home, the five remaining members of the Krew are scattered around the pews. Their families sit in sagging clumps, near to each other, quietly sniffling.

A priest with a face like an old wooden post recites Bible verses that just don't seem to cut it. Don't actually offer an ounce of solace. The casket with Vincent's body is closed. Reignbow, sitting in the back row, sighs with frustration. There's no answers for her here, no answers about nothing. She stands and walks out.

Francisco turns his head and watches her go.

Outside the church, Reignbow takes a big breath of air. A garbage-filled Dumpster reeks nearby. She reaches into her pocket and pulls out a lollipop, sticks it in her mouth. People walking by notice her black dress, then they see the hearse parked out front, and give her a sad stare. One teenager chooses to stop and ask, "Who died, girl?"

"A friend of mine," she says. "A really good friend."

"My condolences, yo. . . ."

Reignbow mutters thanks. The smell of garbage and exhaust intensifies as the sun rises and the day gets hotter. Reignbow crunches down on the lollipop and throws the stick into the gutter.

This place is a disaster, she thinks.

She looks down the block and sees some city construction workers, a rare sight in the ghetto. The workers are on a crane that's floating over an intersection—it's the intersection with the busted traffic light. The workers are fixing the light, installing new bulbs and reflectors. Meanwhile, a cop stands in the middle of the intersection, directing traffic.

Reignbow smiles. She thinks about Detective Keating. She thinks about the bet she lost and how she'll have to trust someone now—Francisco, by the cop's silly rules. Then she thinks about Vincent. She imagines his body resting inside the casket. He's dressed in his best suit, looking handsome. She imagines him peaceful, relaxed, even happy. She imagines his soul taking flight out of the church. He's up above her somewhere, flying over the neighborhood, dodging in and out of the power lines and laughing like crazy.

Reignbow looks up into the sky and smiles. Vincent flies past her and makes his way over the intersection where the traffic light is being repaired. He calls out to the construction workers, who can't hear him.

"Hey, this place is gettin' nice. It's gettin' fixed up! Lookin' good!"

Then Vincent flies on farther, out over the river, racing to the top of Manhattan, and then flying beyond the boroughs far up the Hudson River, all the way till he arrives at Francisco's school—and then, without missing a beat, he continues on, much farther than Vincent ever imagined he'd go in his life, crossing over the ocean and disappearing into the beauty, the quiet, and the calm of the clouds above the sea.

66

Reignbow's housing project pushes up into the evening sky. Soft red clouds encircle the building.

At her apartment door, a black man holds bags of Chinese food. Reignbow hands him a crumpled wad of bills, says thank you, and shuts the door. The other kids of the Krew donate a few bucks to Reignbow, their share of the Chinese. Francisco stands off to the side. Noticeably—to her, at least—he doesn't offer any money. Reignbow deflates a little.

She deposits the bags of food onto the stovetop. Boondangle begins sorting through the paper plates and plasticware. Dinky walks into the kitchen and shuttles cartons of food to where there's some space on top of the microwave. Jason sniffs in the boxes, to see what's what, while Francisco stands back and plays with his tie.

Lily is out at some restaurant, they heard, with Viviana, the two women looking after Vincent's mom. Consoling her. So the kids have run of the apartment.

They take their plates of food and sit around the corner couches of the living room. Wearing black suits and dresses, they all look nice. Someone lights a glass-encased candle that bears a portrait of Jesus, surrounded by cherubs. Set beside the candle are pictures of Vincent as a young boy. A crucifix is laid out. On top of a dresser are flowers and stuffed bears wrapped in cellophane.

Back in the kitchen, Reignbow piles Chinese food onto her plate. Fried rice. Egg rolls. Wings. She's the last to take food. Everyone else is already eating in the living room, except for her and Francisco. Francisco lingers beside her; she looks up, and they stare. She can't tell if it's a good stare or a bad one. Mostly, it's just strange.

"Reign . . ."

"Uh-huh."

"Here's my share for the food. The food . . . and everything else."

He pulls a thick wad of bills out of his pocket. It looks to be about five hundred dollars. Reignbow stares at the money for a moment. He pushes it at her and she finally, almost reluctantly, takes it.

"Thanks," she says simply.

"I messed up so bad with you."

"I know."

"Do you forgive me?"

Reignbow looks up. "You never learn, do you?"

"Learn what?"

"Unless you apologize first, there's nothing for the other person to forgive. Get it?"

"Yeah."

"So . . . ?"

"So, Reign." He puts his hand on her cheek. "Yo. I am so sorry. I am so sorry for lying to you. I'm sorry for walking out on you. I'm sorry . . ." He scratches his head. "There's more. I know it. I just can't think of it all right now."

Reignbow nods. "Yeah, there's a lot more."

"Definitely a lot. But you know, the thing is, I'm not a bad guy."

Reignbow gives him a look of deep and intense skepticism.

"I mean it. I'm not a bad guy. I got lost. But I'm not a bad person." He swallows nervously. "I'm telling you the truth, Reign—do you trust me?"

Reignbow's about to say *no*—to walk away from him. But then she remembers her bet with Detective Keating. She slowly nods. "Okay, okay. I trust you. For now."

Then Reignbow feels the warmth of the sun from the window shining around her head. Like a halo. She smiles and starts eating. Francisco watches her for a little while, then he gestures to her plate of wings.

"You gonna eat that right there?"

"Yeah. That's why I put it there."

"Can I have a bite, at least?" he says.

"You can eat yours."

"No, I'd like you to have mine." He gives her his wing. She laughs a little. "And I'd like to have one of yours."

He takes one from Reignbow's plate, and she smiles as they move into the living room.

The Krew, minus one, eat in silence. Jason is on his own, sitting on a wooden chair that creaks when he moves. They can hear the rhythm of his heavy sighs through the squeaks from the chair. Reignbow scans around at the other kids' expressions to see how they're doing. They seem to be doing better than Jason, because he's sadder than anything she's ever seen.

Half an hour later, Dinky stands up. "I gots to go." She looks around. "Nice seeing the Krew again." Boonsie and Jason nod and quickly stand up with her. "We gotta go, also." They head for the door while Francisco sticks behind, taking a last bite of Chinese and putting down the plate. The five of them pass around hugs and kisses and handshakes like delicate ornaments, a bit cautious and formal.

Reign and Francisco watch their friends walk down the corridor to the elevator, but it's hard to feel that they'll be seeing them again anytime soon. "Bye," Reignbow calls out, wondering if she's saying it for good. "Love you."

She closes the door and leans against the wall. Francisco sits down across from her, his cross dropping out of his shirt and swinging freely. They're quiet for a while. Francisco's hands fold around his face to hide everything that he does not want to show. Reignbow stands above him, cool and collected, her thoughts somewhere far off. She hears an ambulance siren screaming its wet, warbling sound.

"So?" she finally says, to break the silence.

"So . . . what?"

"So what do you wanna do now?"

Francisco isn't sure what she means. With the rest of the day? The rest of his life? "I don't know," he says, answering both questions. "I lost everything, Reign."

"Everything?"

"My life upstate. My life down here. Lost my best friend, too. Got nothing left."

"You still got you."

"Please," he says, rolling his eyes.

"Can you still sink a jumper?"

"Yeah. So?"

"You still a whiz at math?"

"Not as much as I thought I was—"

"But better than me, right?"

"Yeah. Probably."

"And I'm pretty damn hot at math."

Francisco grins, then a frown overtakes his face. "That school was my only shot, Reign."

"It was a *good* shot. But not your only shot. You ever miss a shot in a game and go on to win?"

He looks off.

"That's what I'm talking about."

Francisco sits back and closes his eyes. He closes them for so long that Reignbow wonders if he went to sleep.

"You awake?" she says.

"Vincent's dead. And it's my fault."

"It ain't your fault. No more than it's my fault."

He screws up his face. "Why in the world would it be your fault?"

"It isn't. That's what I'm saying. It's just easy to blame

ourselves. But truth is, it's no one's fault, except Boom's and Vincent's."

He rubs his eyes with the palms of his hands. "I've spent so many years looking after Vincent that I don't know what to do now. He meant everything, but he took so much out of me."

"Yeah. And you know what, Francisco?"

"What?"

"He's gone. You did right by him, but he's gone, and you're free."

"I'm free?" he says softly, then shakes off the idea, not ready for it. "Am I free of you, too?"

Reignbow touches his head. "I don't know. Who knows what we lost and what we'll get back. Life's funny."

"Do you think it'll be like it was before with us?"

Reignbow shrugs. "I don't know." Tears fall down her face. Then through the tears, a smile lifts. "But I'm standing here with you right now, aren't I? I mean, at least I'm still standing here. That must mean something."

Francisco reaches over and hugs Reignbow. It's all he can do. His last, best move. Reignbow wraps her arms across his back. She feels him start to cry, feels the sobs as he presses his weight into her. In an instant, he becomes her old Francisco again, holding her like he needs her. Like he wants her. Like he loves her.

A NOTE ABOUT THE BOOK

I believe that a story about a neighborhood should be born out of that neighborhood. Part of what makes New York endlessly fascinating is its abundance of communities, and one community that holds a special allure for me is Spanish Harlem. A few years ago I started making trips there from my home in Fort Greene, Brooklyn, hoping to tell a story about the place. But I wasn't going there to write a book—at least, not yet. I was going there to make a movie.

Let me back up. Before I ever saw Spanish Harlem, I spent three years working in Hollywood for director Ron Howard. I was involved in the development of movies such as *A Beautiful Mind* and *How the Grinch Stole Christmas*. They were exciting movies to work on, but I yearned to make films that came not from development teams sitting in offices but from real people living in the streets. So I moved to New York and started thinking about the experiences that some friends and I had of going to boarding school and (in my case, as a white scholarship student) feeling like outsiders. After discovering Spanish Harlem and believing that this would be the right community in which to base my story, I created a writing workshop for seven teenagers in the neighborhood. I used writing exercises to bring the teens closer to the material, and to bring me closer to their community. Once I finished the screenplay, I acquired some funding and took the script and teens (who were all non-professional actors) into the streets and shot the film.

Making movies is hard. Guerilla filmmaking (shooting without permits and improvising locations and sudden script changes) comes with its own special challenges. At the time, I was warned by several teachers that half the kids would drop out in the first month. A year later, though, I hadn't lost a single one. Month after month as we moved through Spanish Harlem filming our scenes, packs of curious kids followed us. I put them to work on the crew, and cast several more in the film. The police never bothered us, although we did get thrown off one block by some gang members who didn't want us filming on "their" block. The community, the good and bad of it, infused itself into the story I was telling.

The movie—called *Up with Me*—premiered at the South by Southwest Film Festival. We were able to bring several of the teens to the festival in Austin, Texas, where we won the Special Jury Award for Best Ensemble Cast. We were interviewed by Tavis Smiley on his nationally syndicated radio show, and reviewed glowingly in *O, The Oprah Magazine*, as well as other publications.

Although the Independent Film Channel acquired and released the film, where it enjoyed a successful run, I still didn't feel that the story was finished being told. Using the movie as a jumping-off point, I set out to write a book that captured the feelings of the community, but that also rounded out the original screenplay with new themes and scenes that I didn't have the money to shoot. On our leanest days, *Up with Me* had a crew of two people (including me) and a budget that amounted to pocket change, so it simply wasn't feasible to fill a gymnasium with extras and start pulling off stunts, such as Francisco's fight sequence on the basketball court. Also, with the film's run-time of eighty minutes, there wasn't the luxury of exploring all the plot's nooks and crannies that I could in a novel. Screenwriters often keep a running budget in their heads as they work, pricing out every scene they write. Novelists have the freedom of an infinite budget.

However, this doesn't mean that turning a movie into a novel is easy. The novel may give a writer more "elbow room" to tell her or his story, but movies have the advantage of music, cinematography, set design, wardrobe, and—most important— the performances of gifted actors to convey the emotions of a scene. Certain bits of magic from *Up with Me* would have been impossible to re-create in *When We Wuz Famous*, so scenes needed to be reimagined to work correctly as prose—or be deleted entirely. For instance, there's a scene in the film where the main characters reunite in a park after a long time apart from one another. In the film, the scene is brief, impressionistic, and romantic; the mood is quiet, as the chiaroscuro cinematography and raw performances carry the weight of that scene. In the book, however, I had to create an entirely new structure for the scene, and buttress it with more dialogue and backstory, in order to create that same emotion. The bigger canvas of a book can also sometimes mean more work to fill those open spaces.

I wrote the first draft of *When We Wuz Famous* on my

iPhone, while on my way to work or to pick up my children from school. Adaptations from books to films are a common phenomenon; the results are, famously, mixed. But adaptations that go the other way, from film to book—corny "novelizations" aside—offer the chance to explore visceral, cinematic stories with all the depth and expansiveness that make reading books such an enjoyable, immersive experience. From the streets to the screen to the page, *When We Wuz Famous* is an enduring story for me, of its two teenaged leads, Francisco and Reignbow. Tackling this tale as both a film and a book was less satisfying for the similarities between the two media than for how the image and written word tell stories—and connect with audiences—in such vastly different ways.

ACKNOWLEDGMENTS

The path to this book has been unlikely, and the people who have helped, extraordinary. I owe deep gratitude to my agent, Ryan Fischer-Harbage, who took me in when I had nothing but a manuscript typed into my phone, and for doing what no other agent could. I have such profound appreciation for my editor, Christy Ottaviano, whose warmth and intelligence guided this book from something promising to something I love.

When We Wuz Famous was inspired by a film I made, *Up with Me*, which itself was made as an act of faith by many good and brave people working with me. Among them, six wonderful and brilliant young adults: Francisco Vicioso, Erika Rivera, Brandon Thorpe, Bernice Veloz, Destiny Waters, and Justin Coltrain.

Thanks must be given to my brother, Tom Takoudes, whose early conversations on the topic of this book helped immeasurably in its development, and to the rest of my family for their love and support as I took a path in life far from anything familiar for any of us: Lynda, Christina, George, Andrew, Lisa, and Tamara. To my dad, Christos, whose own path—though it ended almost a decade ago—has inspired two generations and counting.

A writer's life may be rich on the inside, but there's not always a lot of visible glamour from the outside, so true thanks to Sue and Chazz Salkin and Wanda Simpson, for their patience and support.

Finally, for cheering me on when I felt I had no voice with which to write, and for encouraging me when I wasn't sure I deserved it, my family and my core: Emily, Max, and Sadie.